HARVEY
DREW
AND THE JUNK SKUNKS

30131 05361957 0
LONDON BOROUGH OF BARNET

HARVEY DREW AND THE JUNK SKUNKS

CAS LESTER

Illustrations by

SAM HEARN

HOT KEY BOOKS

First published in Great Britain in 2015 by Hot Key Books
Northburgh House, 10 Northburgh Street, London EC1V 0AT

A CIP catalogue record for this book is available from the British Library.

ISBN: 978-1-4714-0334-7

1

This book is typeset in 14pt Sabon using Atomik ePublisher

Printed and bound by Clays Ltd, St Ives Plc

www.hotkeybooks.com

Hot Key Books is part of the Bonnier Publishing Group
www.bonnierpublishing.com

Also By Cas Lester

Harvey Drew and the Bin Men from Outer Space
Harvey Drew and the Bling Bots

Nixie the Bad, Bad Fairy

For the Bin Men of Britain – with sincere thanks, because without you we'd all be in a terrible mess

CHAPTER ONE

The grubbiest galaxy in the Entire Known Universe, and Beyond

THWUMP!

A pair of stonkingly filthy space boots walloped down onto the garbage control desk of the spaceship *Toxic Spew*. They were full of Chief Rubbish Officer Scrummage's feet. Which, in all honesty, were even more revoltingly filthy than his boots. And even smellier than the spaceship. And that says a lot.

'Captain!' protested Senior Engineering Officer Gizmo. 'Must we put up with such slobby manners on the command bridge?' He sneered arrogantly down his hooked nose at his fellow officer. 'He's smearing grime all over the surface!'

As a matter of fact, it was more that Scrummage's boots were mixing *new grime* with the disgusting cocktail of grease and muck that already covered the garbage desk – and, frankly, every other surface, corner and inch of the ship as well. But hey, let's not be picky about this. Anyhow, it was a greenish slimy grime and I don't even want to think about where it might have come from.

To be fair, Chief Rubbish Officer Scrummage was, at the same time, also operating a bit of very complicated, high-tech, galaxy-class space equipment – a vacuum cleaner.

Because the *Toxic Spew* is the plucky little rubbish ship whose five-year mission is to collect all the intergalactic garbage from Galaxy 43b.

It's a hopeless task because that particular far-flung corner of the universe is littered with space trash and is unimaginably filthy.

(No, listen, you're from Earth, so I bet you've never even left your planet on a day trip into outer space. So you have no idea what it's like in the rest of the universe, have you?

This'll help – imagine your home was in space, and you chucked all your waste out of the window – and I mean all of it – even the stuff that goes down the loo. Gross.

Now you can picture Galaxy 43b.

It's officially the grubbiest galaxy in the Entire Known Universe, and Beyond.

And Guess what – the Toxic Spew is officially the grubbiest spaceship in the Entire Known Universe, and Beyond.

And don't even ask about the crew.)

Scrummage was busily – no, make that lazily and sloppily – operating the ship's Ultrawave

3.2 Vacuum Pump and sucking up a pool of grossly gloopy space glop that was slurping around just in front of the ship. It was a dead easy job and a bit boring, so Scrummage had set the pump controls to Super Nova Nozzle Plus and flicked it on to Auto-Suck, and he didn't see why he shouldn't put his filthy feet up on his filthy control desk and relax at the same time.

'Like a bit of extra dirt's going to make a difference!' snorted Pilot Officer Maxie from the flight controls and grinning at the captain from under her multi-coloured fringe.

The grubbiest spaceship in the Entire Known Universe, and Beyond

Captain Harvey Drew looked around the repulsively grubby command bridge of the little Class 4 Intergalactic Garbage Ship. The deck and control desks were littered with, well, litter – chocolate wrappers, pizza crusts, rotting apple cores and something that looked as though it might have once been a lump of gherkin. But then again, it might not.

The surfaces were all generously coated with sticky grunge, and sweaty black mould grew on the walls. It was gross. Frankly, it was beyond gross. In all his eleven years he'd never seen anything so revolting.

(I should probably explain that when I say 'In all his eleven years' I don't mean he's been a spaceship captain for eleven years. It's that Harvey is eleven.

You're probably wondering how an eleven-year-old boy gets to be captain of a spaceship.

I haven't got time to explain that right now.

Sorry.)

'Anyhow what does it matter as long as Scrummage is doing his job?' added Maxie.

She only said it to wind Gizmo up. It worked. His turquoise eyes glared at her from under his white eyebrows and his purple face turned pale lilac. It didn't suit him.

(It might interest you to know, that on Planet Zeryx Minor, which is the home planet of officers Gizmo, Maxie and Scrummage, everyone has multi-coloured hair, turquoise eyes and purple skin.

But then again, given how little you Earth folks get out and about in outer space, it probably won't interest you at all.

Honestly, what are you like?)

'Maxie's right,' said Harvey, brushing his floppy red hair out of his eyes and leaning forward in the tatty black captain's chair. Through the huge vision screens at the front of the bridge, he watched the giant hose of the vacuum pump slurping away and sucking up the space glop. 'As long as the job's getting done.'

'Yup!' said Scrummage smugly, with his feet still on the desk and his huge belly straining his overalls to breaking point. 'It'll soon be finished.'

But then again, maybe it wouldn't. Because suddenly

WHOOP! WHOOP! WHOOP!

all the alarms on the garbage desk went off.

CHAPTER TWO

Flickering spew! There's a blockage!

Harvey watched fascinated, and then horrified, as the giant vacuum hose bulged like a boa constrictor swallowing an outsize rhinoceros, and started juddering violently.

Orange warning lights flashed around the bridge, making it look even more ghastly than usual.

'Flickering spew!' cried Scrummage, swinging his legs off the desk and jumping to his feet. 'There's a blockage!'

He hitched up his overalls over his outsized belly and raced off the bridge.

Harvey leapt out of the tatty black captain's chair and followed him, rushing past Officer Yargal who'd just arrived on the bridge.

'I need to speak with you, Captain!' she cried, flailing her six blue tentacles anxiously. Her green slug-like body trembled in alarm and her three yellow googly eyes waggled wildly.

Since Yargal is both the ship's Medical Officer and Ship's Cook, you would think the captain would at least stop and listen to her, especially when she announced, 'It's a matter of life and death!'

(But then she's a Yargillian, and they're well known for being hyper hysterical, mega melodramatic and super sensational.

They are also, officially, the ugliest aliens in the Entire Known Universe, and Beyond. But it's tactless to mention it. So please don't.)

'Back in a minute!' yelled Harvey, who was

used to Officer Yargal being over excited, over emotional and over the top.

(Funnily enough he's not used to her being revoltingly ugly and repulsively slimy. He'll probably never get used to that.)

'Assuming command!' cried Senior Engineering Officer Gizmo pompously, striding to the captain's chair. He never missed a chance to take control of the ship.

'Yeah, yeah! Whatever!' said Maxie, at the flight desk, rolling her eyes. 'Just don't expect me to do anything you say.'

'Pilot Officer Maxie,' snipped Gizmo irritably, 'may I remind you of the Intergalactic Travel and Transport Pact rules and regulations regarding senior officers taking command in the absence of a captain?'

'Again, yeah, yeah, whatever, and don't expect me to do anything you say,' she replied, pushing up her sleeves and glaring at him challengingly, her bright turquoise eyes glittering dangerously. Gizmo flinched.

Although Maxie wasn't much older than Harvey, she was a brilliant pilot and the only one who could actually fly the *Toxic Spew* and she didn't like being bossed about by a snotty Senior Engineering Officer like Gizmo. Actually, she didn't like being bossed about by anyone.

Gizmo sniffed pompously, settled himself into the captain's chair, and chose to ignore her.

Yargal was lumbering off after Harvey, her single snail-like foot leaving a glistening slime trail across the deck as she went. Several seconds later she'd still only just reached the doors.

Everything under control - or not!

Scrummage ran remarkably quickly for a man who claimed everything was under control. He also ran remarkably quickly for a man of his stature and size (which is a polite way of saying he was short and fat) not to mention remarkably quickly for someone running along the treacherously slippery and slimy floors of the *Toxic Spew*.

Moments later, he and Harvey pelted into the Vacuum Control Centre, down in the hold of the spaceship. Red lights flashed furiously on the pump machine next to three warning symbols:

- an exclamation mark,
- a skull,
- and what looked horribly like a picture of an explosion.

'What do those mean?' Harvey hardly dared to ask.

'No idea!' said Scrummage.

'Seriously?!' gasped Harvey, staggered at how little Scrummage knew about the garbage collection kit. Staggered, but not surprised.

'There must be a user manual somewhere!' exclaimed Harvey, rapidly looking around for one.

VAC-O
MATIC

There wasn't.

Scrummage strode up to the machine, then fearlessly ignoring the flashing warning sign on the top that read:

IN EVENT OF BLOCKAGE
DO NOT REMOVE COVER

he removed the cover. Did I say 'fearlessly'? I think I should have said 'foolishly', because . . .

KA-BOOM!

CHAPTER THREE

Fluttering vomit!

There was an ominous explosion and the end of the hose shot off the Ultrawave 3.2 Vacuum Pump, spewing foul smelling toxic gloop everywhere.

KERSPLAT!

Half the control room, and most of Harvey, was plastered in slimy gunk, and a huge dollop of goo-covered space junk crashed onto the floor.

'Whatever you do, don't lick your lips!'

warned Scrummage urgently, who had (remarkably) managed to stay clear of the mess.

'Space gloop is horribly toxic and if you swallow any your guts will fill with gas and you'll blow up like a balloon!' he added. Then, eyeing the pile of trash on the floor he cried, 'Fluttering vomit! No wonder the hose got blocked!'

Harvey surveyed the heap of garbage. An odd round lump caught his eye. Cautiously he gave it a tap with his foot. It rolled.

'It's a football!' he exclaimed in disbelief, but through firmly clenched teeth. Harvey really missed football. Back home he was used to playing every single day, but he hadn't had a kick-about since he'd left Earth and stopped being the captain of the Highford All Stars and become the captain of the *Toxic Spew* instead.

(You might be wondering how he went from being the captain of a football team to being the captain of a spaceship . . . and I don't blame you.

But, sorry, I still haven't got time to explain.)

'How on Earth did a football get into outer space?' wondered Harvey.

(I hate to be picky. But that is a ridiculous question.

Because, obviously, the football couldn't be both on Earth and in outer space at the same time.)

There was another smaller round object in the junk.

Harvey peered at it. 'Is that a tennis ball?'

Scrummage examined it closely. 'Flickering chunder!' he yelped, panic-stricken. 'That's the planet Microscopica Minor – the tiniest planet in the Entire Known Universe, and Beyond. We're going to have to put that back. We'll get into terrible trouble if the Intergalactic Traffic Police find out we've sucked that up!'

Anxiously he prodded around to see what else they'd vacuumed aboard by mistake.

'That's the rear-end grill of a subsonic head gasket,' he announced, pointing to a rusty bit of metal that had broken off another spaceship. 'If I clean that up it might be useful! And look!' he cried excitedly, picking up a bit of tatty old computer equipment. 'That's the Wi-Fi control panel from the *Toxic Spew*! Gizmo will be well chuffed!'

'Please tell me you're joking,' said Harvey in disbelief, keeping his lips as still as possible.

(Which is actually incredibly difficult. And, in the interests of being accurate, I should probably say that what he actually said was 'Leez tell ne you're yoking.')

Scrummage goes all soppy

The rest of the junk was mostly pretty unidentifiable except for a couple of empty pizza boxes and what looked like a large bright orange egg. It was cracked. Actually, it was in the middle of cracking, and right before their very eyes.

'Er . . . Scrummage,' said Harvey nervously, 'what's that?'

(Look, I'm sorry to keep interrupting, but I don't want to suggest that Harvey is the nervous type. It's just that in the short time he's been on the Toxic Spew, he's learnt to be wary of any alien life forms you find in space trash.

You know, like poisonous pink killer maggots from Venomoid Flux who inject you with poison, melt your insides and suck up your innards like soup.

You've got to admit, he's got a point.)

As he looked at the egg, Scrummage's face softened and went all soppy. 'Ahhhhh,' he cooed. 'It's a baby Gordonzola . . . and it's hatching!' Gently he scooped it up. 'I'm going

to keep it,' he announced, adding proudly, 'I'm going to call it Gordon!'

Harvey was just about to ask what a Gordonzola was and whether it was actually wise to keep one, when Yargal arrived, trembling with exhaustion.

'Captain, it really is urgent!' she panted.

(Since the story has just got to a quite interesting bit, you'd probably prefer it if I told you more about the Gordonzola at another time, wouldn't you?

That's the problem with you Earth people. You're just not really interested in other life forms, are you?)

A dribble of space gloop was just oozing between Harvey's lips so he dashed off to his quarters to clean up, promising Yargal he'd meet her on the bridge afterwards. Scrummage gently put the Gordonzola, still in its egg, safely out of harm's way, and set about trying to fix the hose back onto the Ultrawave 3.2 Vacuum Pump.

Yargal sighed wearily and slithered off again. Even though she hurried straight to the bridge as fast as her slippery sucky foot would let her, and she didn't stop to:

- shower, or
- change her uniform, or
- grab a handful of jellybeans (like Harvey did, from the machine in his quarters), he actually got back to the bridge before she did.

'Captain,' she puffed, finally catching up with him, 'I have . . . something terrible . . . to tell you . . .'

But before she could finish, Scrummage radioed up and interrupted her.

(I bet you're desperate to know what Yargal needs to tell Harvey. Well, you're just going to have to wait until the next chapter.

Bad luck.)

CHAPTER FOUR

Gobsmacked

Harvey was gobsmacked to hear Scrummage ask Gizmo's advice. The two officers were constantly slinging insults, hurling punches and aiming occasional kicks at each other. Before Harvey joined them, they'd waged a constant 'battle for the command of the ship' with Maxie caught in the middle. It was chaos.

'Gizmo, I'm re-attaching the vacuum hose duct onto the pump flange tube,' said Scrummage. Harvey listened carefully hoping to pick up some technical tips.

'Which sticky tape should I use?' continued Scrummage. 'The red one or the green and yellow stripy one?'

Harvey was gobwalloped! 'Hang on! You're not seriously going to repair the galaxy-class Ultrawave 3.2 Vacuum Pump with *a bit of sticky tape*?'

'Um . . . there isn't anything else,' cringed Gizmo.

Maxie snorted with laughter.

Yargal tried to get Harvey's attention. 'Captain . . .' she said.

'Not now, Yargal,' replied Harvey. Looking around the bridge, he saw that loads of vital controls and key bits of kit were held together by sticky tape.

'Is that the standard repair kit for the *Toxic Spew*?' he asked witheringly. 'A couple of rolls of sticky tape?'

'Er . . . no,' admitted Gizmo, thoroughly embarrassed.

'Captain . . .' tried Yargal again, more urgently.

'Not now, Yargal!' barked Harvey.

'Excuse me, Captain,' said the computer smugly. 'But I know for a fact that the *Toxic Spew* was issued with the standard repair equipment when it launched on its current mission.

(Is it helpful for me to remind you that the Class 4 Intergalactic Garbage Ship is on a five-year mission to collect all the rubbish in Galaxy 43b?

Probably not. But then you didn't have to read that bit if you didn't want to, did you?

So don't blame me.)

'But the crew have managed to lose the entire contents of the tool kit,' the computer went on. 'Of course, it's not their fault. They can't help being the sloppiest, laziest, most useless and careless, disgraceful, rubbish crew in the Entire Known Universe, and Beyond,' it finished.

'We're a garbage crew, not a 'rubbish' crew!' growled Scrummage furiously through the intercom.

'I said 'rubbish' and I meant 'rubbish!' snipped the computer.

Gizmo winced and even Maxie kept her head down.

'The *Toxic Spew*,' continued the computer importantly, 'should be carrying a fully functioning utility kit including:

- A wiffometer, to detect whether the smell of the garbage is:

  a) hazardously horrendous, or
  b) dangerously disgusting, or
  c) fatally foul

and

- A reinforced rubber toilet plunger;
- And one of those little scratch remover pens that are so handy for repairing all

the little scrapes and nicks on the outside of the ship.

It hardly seems worth it, thought Harvey, *given the rusty, tatty and battered state of the ship's exterior.*

A sudden thought occurred to Harvey.

'Is there a ship's manual on your system?'

'Do you mean a complete breakdown of all the parts of the ship, how they work, how to use them, how to repair them and so on?' asked the computer.

'Yes!' said Harvey excitedly.

'No!' it said.

Harvey sighed.

Yargal was still hovering breathlessly by the captain's chair, desperate to speak with him. Harvey finally asked what she wanted.

'Captain!' she replied dramatically and waggling her six blue tentacles importantly. 'It's a matter of life and death. As Ship's Cook it is my duty to inform you that we have almost completely run out of food! And, as the ship's

Medical Officer it is my duty to inform you, and I do hate to mention it now, when I know you have a lot of other things to worry about, but we're all going to die!'

CHAPTER FIVE

Captain! This is a disaster!

Harvey was used to Yargal violently over-reacting at the slightest opportunity. Honestly, if he'd had a point for every time she'd melodramatically flounced onto the command bridge, feverishly flinging blue tentacles and grey snot around liberally, he'd be at the top of the Premier League by now.

But he was gobstruck by the panic-stricken responses of Maxie and Gizmo.

'Captain! This is a disaster!' sobbed Gizmo hysterically, bursting into tears, pacing up and down the deck, and wringing his hands.

'Pull yourself together, Officer Gizmo!' barked Harvey. 'Calm down, settle down and sit down! And that's an order!'

Gulping and hiccupping, the Senior Engineering Officer collapsed weeping into his seat.

'For crying out loud, Harvey!' snapped Maxie from the flight deck. 'I don't think you understand the dreadfully dire and desperate dangerousness of our plight, or the alarmingly awful and appalling atrociousness of the situation!' she finished, yelling at full volume.

'Have you finished, Officer Maxie?' asked Harvey evenly. Maxie hadn't.

'Let me explain, Earth Boy!' she said pushing up her sleeves, marching over to him, and shoving her bright purple face into his and speaking *painfully loudly.* 'We are stuck in a tiny spaceship in a remote corner of Galaxy 43b and WE – HAVE – NO – FOOD! We're not talking about feeling a bit peckish, or fancying a little snack or wondering if there's a packet of cheese and onion crisps or tin of assorted toffees left in the back of the galley cupboard! WE ARE GOING TO STARVE TO DEATH! Fine captain you're turning out to be! What are we supposed to eat?' she demanded furiously.

'How about each other?' suggested the computer cheerfully.

Too young to be eaten!

'Aaaaargh!' screamed Yargal. 'Captain, I'm too young to be eaten! Save me!' she sobbed, flinging her soggy tentacles around Harvey. Long strings of grey slime dribbled from her nostrils onto his uniform.

'Steady, Officer Yargal,' he said calmly, and gently but firmly peeling her off him. 'No one is going to eat anyone else.'

Yargal stood shaking like a green and blue jelly slug, with grey snot dribbling down her slimy body and pooling onto the deck.

Secretly Harvey couldn't imagine anybody

wanting to eat anything as revolting as Yargal, but he was much too polite to say so.

Harvey snapped at the computer. 'If you can't say anything useful, then just . . . don't say anything!'

'But that was useful,' retorted the computer. 'The crew will probably kill each other anyway,' it muttered sulkily.

'Scrummage will definitely murder Yargal when he finds out there's no food,' announced Maxie.

'Captain! I'm too young to be murdered!' wailed Yargal.

Scrummage, of course, was still in the Vacuum Control Centre, trying to fix the hose back onto the pump machine with sticky tape, and hadn't heard the grim news. Well, not yet, he hadn't.

(I don't know about you, but I'm looking forward to the moment when he does. That'll be a high point.)

Calming Yargal down, Harvey told her to

follow him to the galley so he could see the state of the food supplies for himself.

'Assuming command,' sniffed Gizmo, going over to the captain's chair, trying to stop snivelling, and drying his tears on his sleeves.

'Really?' queried Maxie witheringly. It was bad enough being bossed around by an arrogant, pompous Senior Engineering Officer, but a weepy, blubbing, sniffing one was off-the-scale of even worse.

Gross-out in the galley

It won't surprise you to know that the galley of the *Toxic Spew* was indescribably gross. Smears of mouldy mozzarella and tomato sauce plastered the walls, the floor and even the ceiling. An interesting mildew-coloured fungus was actually growing out of one of the store cupboards. At least Harvey assumed it was a fungus. It might have been an alien friend of Yargal's – he didn't like to ask.

The smell in the kitchen was unbelievably atrocious. Harvey covered his nose and mouth with his hands and tried to breathe as little as possible. A heap of rotting leftover food festered in one corner, maggots squirming all over it.

'Isn't there a waste bin?' choked Harvey, as soon as Yargal slithered into the galley after him.

'No,' she replied. 'But that,' she added proudly, pointing to a trapdoor under the pile of rotten food, 'is a rubbish chute. It goes straight down into the garbage hold. Watch this!' She pulled a lever and the hatch flipped open and the food tumbled down.

Harvey would have been impressed, but he was nearly knocked out by the terrible stench of decaying vegetables and foul drains that wafted up, and he gagged.

'Sorry, sir,' said Yargal. 'Is it a bit smelly? We Yargillions don't have much sense of smell.'

Well, that explains a lot, thought Harvey.

Opening the cupboards, Yargal showed Harvey the pitiful remains of the food supplies – empty tubs labelled tomato paste, glacé cherries, anchovies, pickled onions and so on, and then she proudly presented the pizza maker. There were several other food machines in the galley, but Yargal told Harvey she didn't know how to use them and there weren't any instruction manuals. The pizza machine was dead easy because, although it was covered in buttons and complicated dials, it was voice controlled – so Yargal simply had to tell it what to make.

They'd had to programme it so that it only recognised her voice because Scrummage had kept sneaking into the galley and pigging out on pizza all day and night.

Harvey went over to one of the others. It was labelled 'PopUpPuds' and looked a bit like a toaster. He pressed the 'Start' button. It clunked and whirred for a while, then pinged a couple of times and a puff of steam erupted from its side. Harvey watched hopefully, wondering what sort of pudding would emerge. Actually he didn't care – as long as it wasn't rhubarb crumble.

POP
TM
UP PUDS
SPLOO
GLOP

It wasn't.
In fact there wasn't any pudding at all.
There was, however, an impressive

WHOOOMPH!

as the PopUpPuds machine burst into flames.

CHAPTER SIX

Bad news

Thick black smoke poured out, sending the fire alarm and sprinkler systems into full-on panic-overdrive mode,

SPRAAAAAY!

DRIIIII-IIIING!

and Harvey's overalls were soaked – for the second time that day.

Yargal scraped a bit of gunk off the label above the 'Start' button on the pudding maker.

'DO NOT PRESS RED BUTTON IF FOOD TRAY IS EMPTY', it read.

'Whoops,' said Yargal, sympathetically. 'Good job I'm the cook, and you're not!' Then, looking around the galley she added 'I think I can just about scrape together enough food to make a small pizza for lunch.'

Following her gaze around the filthy, food-splattered room, Harvey didn't like to think what she might actually scrape up. But he left her to it and waddled off soggily to put on another set of clothes. At this rate he'd be wearing his school uniform by lunchtime.

(If you're one of those bright sparks who don't miss much, then you're probably wondering why Harvey's got his school clothes with him.

If you're not, or, if you already know, then you can skip the next bit.

Harvey was wearing his school uniform when he accidentally applied for the job of Captain of the Toxic Spew. He picked

up a message from aliens on the computer in his bedroom, but he couldn't understand it because it looked like this:

To: ↳⇔◢↕⇔⇨ ↓⇔ ◀↑⇨ ⇨⇔◀↓△⇨ ⇊⇔↕▷⇔ ⌥⇔↓◁⇨△▽⇨⤓ ⇨⇔⇦ ⇥⇨◢↕⇔⇦

But that didn't stop him replying – and getting transported onto the command bridge of the Toxic Spew – still in his school uniform.)

When he'd been on Earth, and captain of the Highford All Stars, Harvey often had to break bad news to his team. Like when their goalie got stolen by another club, and when their best striker broke his toe and couldn't play for the rest of the season, and worst of all, when his mum accidentally dyed their kit bubblegum pink.

So when he got back to the bridge he took a deep breath and courageously announced, 'There's nothing left to eat except a small pizza.'

'Oh good grief!' gulped Gizmo tragically.

'Whatever you do, don't tell Scrummage,' warned Maxie.

'Don't tell Scrummage what?' asked Scrummage walking onto the bridge, the doors schwooshing open and closing automatically as he did so.

Bad taste

There was an awkward silence, broken by Yargal arriving, and the doors doing the schwooshing thing again. Yargal was carrying a pitifully small pizza – actually it was a *dangerously* small pizza. She was quaking so much she nearly dropped it. Snuffles, the ship's huge Hazard Hunting Hound, lolloped along beside her, drooling hopefully, his huge shark-like teeth drenched in saliva.

'I know it's rather small, but it's *packed* with flavour!' she quavered, and taking a deep breath went on. 'It's fried asparagus (only slightly rotten), soggy Brussels sprouts, bacon-flavoured ice cream, and burnt sweetcorn slop, topped with squished bananas, crispy burnt marshmallows and hot chillies smothered in chocolate. And there's a sloppy orange and cheese stuffed crust!' she finished despairingly.

Scrummage looked slowly from the pizza to Yargal and back again. 'Is that all there is for lunch?!' he snarled, going an alarming shade of dark purple.

'No, that's all there is to eat – *at all!*' stated Maxie.

'And it's for *everyone*,' growled Gizmo pointedly at Scrummage.

Harvey was just about to give up his share of the pizza when the computer bleeped cheerfully.

'Captain,' it said, 'I've had a brilliant idea.'

Phew! thought Harvey, who was becoming distinctly worried by the way Scrummage and Gizmo were glaring at each other . . . hungrily.

The computer continued brightly. 'Why not throw some of the crew off the ship? Then there'll be more pizza for those who are left!'

'WHAT!?' spluttered Harvey, horrified.

An astonishingly shocking row immediately erupted.

(It was so bad, I couldn't put all of it here. I've just kept some of the least unpleasant bits.)

'You can't throw me off! I'm the only one who can fly the ship!' yelled Maxie fiercely.

Gizmo grabbed Snuffles menacingly by the collar. 'The hound can go for a start! He's not exactly useful!'

'Yes he is!' cried Yargal hotly, thwacking Gizmo with her tentacle. 'He does a very important job sniffing out dangerous garbage and he's staying!'

'All right, what about you, then?' retorted Gizmo.

'You can't get rid of me!' wailed Yargal. 'I'm the only one who can cook . . . or deal with any medical emergencies.'

'Well, we need Harvey,' argued Maxie 'Because he's:

a) a good leader and planner,
b) the captain, and
c) the only one who can stop Gizmo and Scrummage from killing each other.'

'Maybe he should let them,' suggested the computer, 'then there'd be two less to feed!'

'Computer! That's enough!' snapped Harvey.

'Looks like it's you two then,' said Maxie glowering at Gizmo and Scrummage, pushing up her sleeves and advancing on them threateningly.

'Maxie!' barked Harvey.

'I say Scrummage goes!' yelled Gizmo. 'He eats more than everyone else put together!'

Scrummage's hands flew round Gizmo's throat, throttling him.

Harvey leapt between them. 'PACK IT IN!' he bawled. 'No one is throwing anyone off the ship! And computer, butt out!'

'I was only trying to help!' it snipped, bleeping off in a massive hissy fit.

The I.S.S.

Harvey took a deep breath and calmly asked Maxie where the nearest place was where they could get some food. There was a moment's silence while she checked on the ship's 3D star map.

'The I.S.S.,' she replied.

Harvey couldn't believe his ears! 'The International Space Station?!' he exclaimed. If the I.S.S. was nearby then they must be close to Earth and he could go home!

'Er, no,' said Maxie confused. 'I.S.S. stands for Intergalactic Super Store. It's called *Waitless*.

Harvey was gutted. But, remembering he was the captain, he pulled himself together and ordered Maxie to plot the course.

'The quickest way to get there is through a black hole,' she replied casually.

'What?!' cried Harvey.

(Harvey might be from a planet that no one in Galaxy 43b has ever heard of, but even he knows that if you go into a black hole you'll die from 'spaghettification' and being stretched ultra-supa-mega-nova thin!)

'It'll take *ages* to get there if we don't,' whined Maxie.

Four pairs of hungry eyes and three anxious googly ones stared at Harvey – dangerously.

Maxie's hands hovered above the flight controls.

'So, Captain, what are we going to do?'

CHAPTER SEVEN

Rumble, grumble

Harvey was torn.

On the one hand, he thought, perhaps he was wrong. Maybe it *wasn't* that dangerous to cut through a black hole, or the crew wouldn't want to do it.

He could hardly claim to be an expert at travelling through black holes in deep space.

(I hate to be rude, but frankly, Harvey could hardly claim to be an expert at travelling through deep space at all.

But then no one on your funny little

blue and green planet can, can they?

It's amazing to think that nobody on Earth has ever been further away than your own tiny little moon.

Just what is it that puts you off space travel? Is it the lack of regular flights? Or the lack of loo paper?

Or the lack of oxygen?

Or is it the food?)

But on the other hand, Harvey knew that his crew could be reckless and greedy and frankly stupid, and it was his job as captain to make the right decision – even if the entire crew disagreed and would end up lynching him.

So he ordered Maxie to take the longer, safer route and everyone groaned loudly. Almost as loudly as their stomachs.

RUMBLE, GRUMBLE

WHINGE, WHINE

'I need *food*!' moaned Scrummage, slumped weakly at the garbage control desk, clutching his outsize belly.

'Stop complaining,' sniffed Gizmo. 'You've got loads of spare fat to use up.'

Maxie snorted rudely. She'd put the ship onto AutoAstronaut and was sitting with her knees pulled up, hugging her empty stomach.

'How dare you!' snarled Scrummage, patting his belly proudly. 'I'd rather have some meat on me than be a scrawny weakling like you!'

'Gentlemen!' warned Harvey. But the two officers launched into an all-out slanging match with insults bouncing round the bridge like ping-pong balls.

'Fatso!' yelled Gizmo.

'Skinny Ribs!'

'That's enough!' cried Harvey. They ignored him.

'Blubber Boy!'

'Scraggy Chops!'

'I'm warning you . . .' threatened Harvey, a dangerous edge to his voice, 'I'm going to count to three and . . . '

'Porker!'

'Weed!'

'Right, that's it!' thundered Harvey. 'Go to your rooms. Er, I mean quarters!'

Gizmo stormed off. It's a good job the *Toxic Spew* is kitted out with sliding doors, otherwise he would have slammed them all so hard they'd have snapped off their hinges.

Harvey had never been in Gizmo's quarters – but if he had, he would have been gobsmacked. They were clean. They were tidy. They were everything the rest of the *Toxic Spew* wasn't. By which I mean they weren't a health hazard.

Gizmo got to his (spotless) quarters, flung himself onto his (creaseless) bed and stared at the (stainless) walls and ceiling. The tidy, sparse room usually had a calming effect on the Senior Engineering Officer.

He sighed and looked around. There was nothing out of place, nothing left out, but also, crucially . . . *nothing to eat!*

He tried to distract himself by memorising The Complete Guide to Intergalactic Travel and Transport Pact Rules and Regulations (Volume 1).

It didn't work.

GROAN, GRUMBLE, GRIPE . . .

went Gizmo's stomach and

GROAN, GRUMBLE, GRIPE . . .

went Gizmo.

Bad Snuffles!

You'll be staggered to hear that as soon as Scrummage stomped into his (astoundingly filthy) quarters he forgot all about his hollow belly.

Because the baby Gordonzola had finally hatched!

Scrummage had slipped the egg into his underwear drawer so it would have somewhere safe to nest when it emerged.

(I don't know about you, but I'm not sure which is the more disgusting thought: Scrummage letting a baby Gordonzola hatch in his undies, or making a baby alien sleep in a pair of Scrummage's huge and grossly grubby boxer shorts.

Oh, yuk.)

Either way, the little alien now sat watching Scrummage with interest. Its little podgy pink body glowed with bright purple spots. Along its back, soft turquoise spines, which would grow into large spikes, lay flattened in its fluffy fur. Scrummage tickled it behind its tiny pink ears and let its green needle-sharp baby teeth gnaw gently at his fat fingers.

'Are you hungry? Come on, ickle Gordon,' he cooed gently, scooping up the baby alien,

'let's see if Aunty Yargal has something you can eat,' and he set off for the galley.

(By the way, if you're finding it difficult to believe that Scrummage would let Gordon eat food, or indeed anything at all, that he could eat himself, you're dead right.

Fortunately, Gordonzolas eat curdled milk, rotten food and maggots – and even Scrummage isn't that desperate.

Well, not yet.)

Uh oh, Hazard Hunting Hound meets Gordonzola

In the galley, Yargal fussed round the new arrival like a midwife.

'He's adorable!' she cried and, scraping up a maggoty lump of soggy pizza crust from the deck with one of her tentacles, she offered it to Gordon who nibbled it cautiously.

Snuffles eyed the food jealously. Then he eyed the Gordonzola suspiciously. In all his multiple intergalactic missions, the huge Hazard Hunting Hound had never come across one before. And he wasn't sure if he could trust it.

It looked cute enough, but in his experience you could never be too careful. He let out a soft, throaty growl and the baby Gordonzola shrank from the sound, whimpering fearfully and flicking up its little spines bravely in self-defence. (Very bravely when you come to think of it, given the size and sheer quantity of Snuffles's teeth. It would be like trying to fight off a Great White Shark with a comb.)

'Steady boy!' said Scrummage to Snuffles, suddenly concerned that the hound might actually attack Gordon.

'Relax! He's only saying "Hello", aren't you?' said Yargal patting Snuffles on the head with a spare tentacle and then adding firmly, 'Now, play nicely!'

Suddenly two enormous grey shaggy paws walloped onto the galley worktop, one either side of Gordon, as the enormous hound stood up on his back legs and eyeballed the baby Gordonzola. Then he put his huge pink meatball of a nose up to the tiny little alien and sniffed it hard – so hard he almost inhaled it.

SNIIIIIIFFFFFF

And then he stuck out his lolloping great tongue, between his horrifically sharp white teeth and licked Gordon gently.

'Ahhhh, look, he likes him,' sighed Scrummage, immensely relieved.

'Good boy,' said Yargal proudly.

Then Snuffles opened his massive mouth and wolfed the little Gordonzola inside.

'NO!' cried Yargal.

CHAPTER EIGHT

Gloomy, grumpy and grouchy on the bridge

'Bad dog!' cried Yargal as Snuffles slunk off with his prize. 'Spit, Snuffles, Spit!' she ordered.

'DROP!' bellowed Scrummage. **'DROP!!!'**

Snuffles gently spat the little alien onto the deck. Then he tenderly nudged Gordon with his nose, and licked him again. The little Gordonzola rubbed its tiny pink and purple face against the hound's huge hairy face.

The Hazard Hunting Hound from Canine Major thumped his tail happily and promptly

adopted Gordon. He'd always wanted puppies.
Scrummage and Yargal sighed in relief.

For the next few hungry hours, everyone kept moaning about their empty bellies – except Harvey who was trying to lead by example. It wasn't working. Eventually, he had to threaten to fine anyone for using any of the following words:

- starving,
- ravenous,
- famished,
- peckish,
- nibble,
- munch,
- crunch,
- slurp and . . . actually, the list was endless, but you get the picture.

Eventually, when there was absolutely no chance of anything for supper and Scrummage had resorted to licking the food-splattered walls of the galley, the crew sloped off to bed hungry and gloomy.

The next morning they woke up even more hungry and gloomy. Not to mention grumpy and grouchy, crabby and cranky, oh, and surly and snappy. They sprawled pathetically in their seats on the command bridge, groaning wretchedly.

(Since you've never been on a spaceship, let alone stuck on one for years on end, you probably can't really grasp the vital importance of meals.

Breaking up the deadly boring routine of collecting intergalactic garbage, they're the high points of the mission.

Which, given Yargal's cooking, says a lot about how much interplanetary bin men enjoy their work.

Tragic, isn't it?)

Dangerously close to mutiny on the bridge

As captain of the Highford All Stars, Harvey knew all about food moods. Or rather 'lack of food' moods as he called them. So he always kept a stash of chocolate bars in his kit bag to boost everyone at half-time. And this morning, at breakfast time, he'd handed out the last of the jellybeans from the machine in his quarters. There were five and a half jellybeans each.

There was *ages* still to go until they got to *Waitless*, and the famished bridge crew were nearly at breaking point.

Harvey knew he had to take their minds off their empty bellies. Which was a sizeable challenge – especially for Scrummage. So he got the crew to list everything they needed from *Waitless*.

Scrummage's list was the longest: as in 'it was the longest list in the history of the Entire Known Universe, and Beyond'. It was all food.

Here's just a tiny bit of it:

- . . . pickles,
- mozzarella,
- garlic crisps,
- hot dogs,
- cake with melted chocolate topping,
- BBQ sauce,
- chocolate chip cookies,
- ice cream (strawberry, vanilla, chocolate, honeycomb and toffee crunch),
- coco star pops,
- scorchios . . .

'What are "scorchios"?' asked Harvey.

'Super-hot chilli-coated crunchy cereal,' explained Yargal.

Yeowch! thought Harvey. *Talk about a hot breakfast!*

Yargal's list was definitely the most surprising:

- kitchen roll,
- loo roll,

- goo-resistant plasters,

and

- a new broom handle.

'The *Toxic Spew* has a broom?' asked Harvey, gobsmacked. 'And someone's actually used it?!'

'Don't be silly,' laughed Maxie. 'Gizmo broke it whacking Scrummage,' and grinning broadly, she handed Harvey her list.

At the top of Maxie's list, and in big letters, was the Retro Look Flash Intergalactic 2000 Steering Wheel, followed by lots of sweets and snacks:

- supanova supasour supasucker gobstoppers,
- space raider crisps,
- double choc space munchies,
- chewy Jupiter jelly mix,

and

- fizzy alien guts (red ones).

'Alien guts?!' cried Harvey, disgusted.

'Yeah, they're slippery, gooey, gungy, rubbery, fruity strings.'

'Yuk!' said Harvey

'Yup!' grinned Maxie.

Gizmo's list included twenty-one bits for the ship, which, to Harvey's alarm, he said were *absolutely vital* to stop the *Toxic Spew* falling apart in mid space. And an Anger Ball for Scrummage.

'Does Scrummage actually want an Anger Ball?' asked Harvey.

'I doubt it. But I'm going to throw it at him and make him angry, anyway,' replied Gizmo.

'No,' said Harvey firmly. 'You are not,' and he deleted it.

It won't surprise you to know that Harvey's list was the most useful:

- protective suit for Snuffles,
- learn how to cook book for Yargal,
- basic spaceship manual,

and

- a dictionary of space illnesses.

(It wasn't that he didn't trust Yargal as Medical Officer to keep him healthy, it was more that he didn't trust Yargal not to accidentally kill him – especially with her cooking.)

But Harvey couldn't distract his hungry crew for long and by mid morning, with no proper breakfast, no chance of elevenses, *and don't even ask about lunch*, they were dangerously close to mutiny!

'Flickering spew! I can't take this any more!' whimpered Scrummage.

'Neither can I!' groaned Gizmo.

'We'd be there by now if we'd taken the shortcut through the black hole,' muttered Maxie darkly. 'This is crazy!'

'This is torture!' growled Gizmo.

'This is agony!' howled Scrummage.

'Pull yourselves together, all of you!' snapped Harvey irritably. 'This is ridiculous!'

'No,' retorted Maxie, pushing up her sleeves and glaring at him challengingly. 'This is *mutiny*!'

CHAPTER NINE

Mutiny on the *Toxic Spew*!

With Gizmo and Scrummage egging her on, Maxie boldly announced she was going to defy Harvey's orders and take the shorter route through the black hole.

'It's only *slightly* dangerous,' she argued.

'It's suicidal!' gasped Harvey. 'What about spaghettification?'

'Do you mean when your entire body gets pushed and pulled and squeezed and stretched, and your brains and bones and all your other important bodily parts are squidged even thinner than a single, solitary piece of spaghetti – and an uncooked piece at that?' she asked.

'Exactly!' cried Harvey.

'It'll be fine,' shrugged Maxie. 'We have an Anti-Pasta Intergalactic Shield 3000!'

(You don't actually have these on your spaceships do you? Honestly, you Earthlings are so primitive.

Here's a quick description of one, and how it works. It's only short, and not very technical, so please do try keep up.

The Anti-Pasta Intergalactic Shield 3000 is in two parts, one on each side of the spaceship. It's basically two flat pieces of metal with lots of tiny holes. They look a bit like gigantic squashed spaghetti sieves, but square.

Stop me if I'm going too fast for you, won't you?

It works by projecting a portal for the ship to fly through, which creates a powerful protective shield around the ship.

Clever, huh?

Bet you wish your poky little planet could invent stuff like that.)

Harvey didn't really have a choice.

'Fine,' he sighed, 'we'll take the shortcut through the black hole,' and the bridge crew cheered.

Maxie had to plot the route herself because the computer was still sulking, but that was probably just as well – the computer's maths is well dodgy.

As they approached the black hole, Maxie confidently hit the big red button on the top of the Anti-Pasta Intergalactic Shield 3000. Through the vast front vision screen Harvey saw a kind of square gateway shimmering up ahead. As the ship passed through it a loud and distinctly disturbing thumping noise started up. It was the anti-pasta shield forming all around the ship.

Harvey gripped the arms of his captain's chair and ordered himself not to panic as the plucky

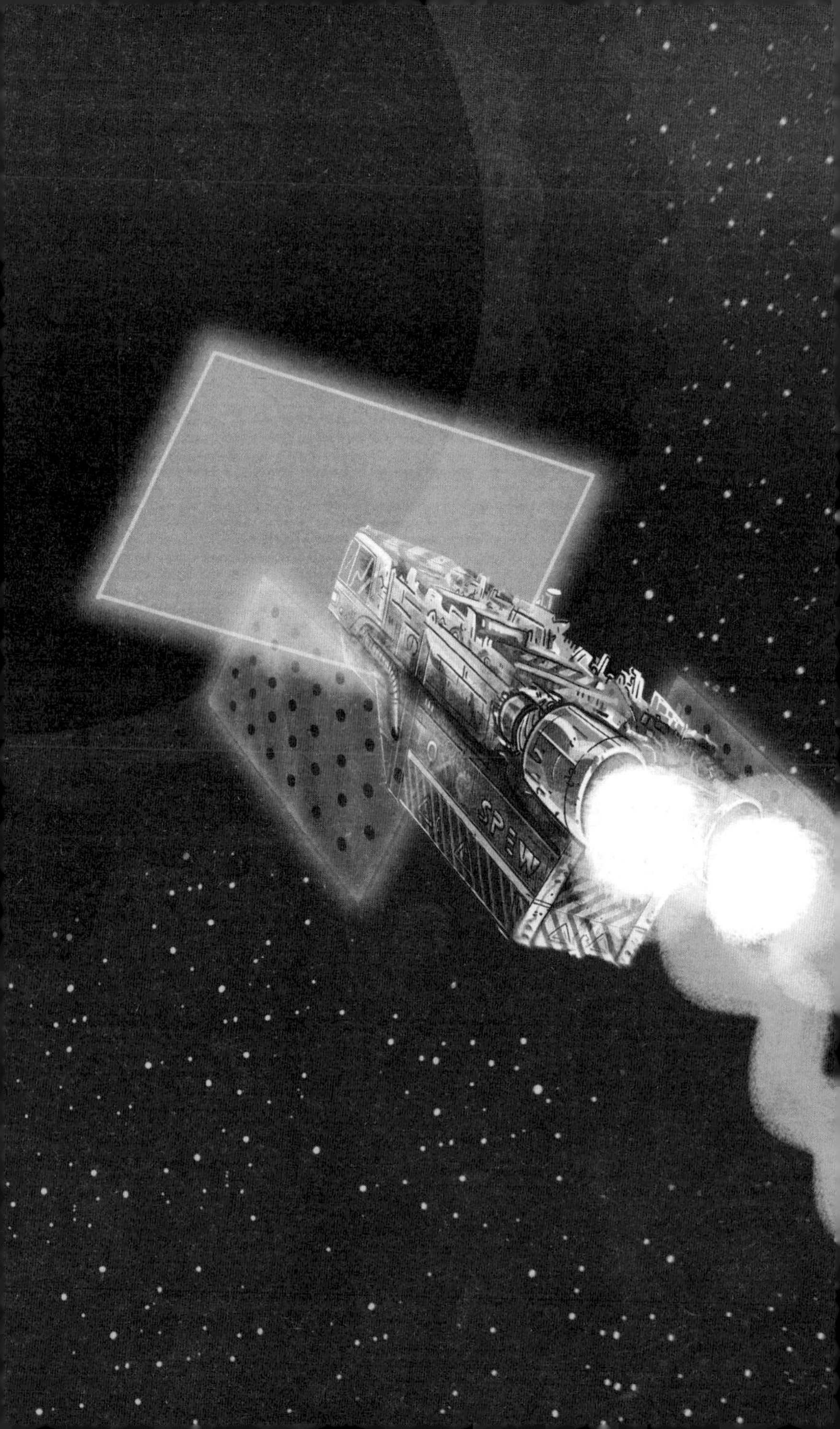
SPEW

little intergalactic garbage ship headed into the terrifying, swirling vortex of nothingness of the black hole! Blimey!

Swirling vortex of nothingness!

Flying into the black hole was like being sucked into the hose of a giant vacuum cleaner and being gobbled up by one of the hungriest beings in the Entire Known Universe, and Beyond – at the same time.

And it was dark. Darker than dark. Even light struggles in a black hole. Time can give up and stop altogether. And of course once you've been pulled into a black hole – it's impossible to get out.

Which was a thought that had occurred to Harvey. But he trusted Maxie and didn't seriously think she'd do anything ridiculously risky, ludicrously lethal or foolishly fatal . . . would she?

(Is it just me, or does it seem a bit late for Harvey to be asking himself that?)

'Hang on,' said Harvey suddenly. 'What did you mean by only "*slightly* dangerous"?'

'Oh, nothing much. It's just that in order to get out of a black hole you need cybersonic jump drive,' replied Maxie.

'Do we have cybersonic jump drive?' asked Harvey.

'No,' said Maxie.

'What!?' cried Harvey.

'Relax! If I put the hydrosonic hyperdrive lever into top gear we should be fine!' She grinned, and her bright turquoise eyes glittered mischievously.

She reached across the flight control desk and hauled on the hydrosonic hyperdrive lever. It promptly snapped off in her hand.

'Oops!' she said.

'Fluttering upchuck!' swore Scrummage.

'Aaaargh!' wailed Yargal.

'What are we going to do?' screeched Gizmo hysterically.

‘Don’t panic!’ ordered Harvey.

‘Why not?’ screamed Gizmo.

Which was a good question because . . . the *Toxic Spew*, and all on board, was spiralling into the absolute and total nothingness of a black hole, completely out of control, and with no way of getting out of it . . .

and they were probably,
literally and
totally . . .
all going to die!

CHAPTER TEN

Total panic on the *Toxic Spew*!

Through the smudged and grimy front vision screen of the *Toxic Spew* the terrified crew stared in horror as they hurtled further and further into the deadly darkness of the black hole with the certain knowledge that they couldn't get out again!

I'll be honest with you – it was total panic on the bridge, with the crew sobbing and screaming and running round like headless er . . . well, I don't like to be tactless, but . . . headless aliens.

'Calm down!' ordered Harvey.

'Why should I?' shrieked Gizmo dramatically and clutching his multi-coloured hair in a frenzy of fear.

'Somebody slap him! He's hysterical!' wailed Yargal, who, frankly, was even more hysterical than Gizmo.

'Bagsy I do it!' begged Scrummage, leaping up eagerly.

'NO!' snapped Harvey. 'Everybody QUIET!' he bellowed.

To his enormous surprise, everyone shut up and settled down, and some sort of order returned to the bridge. Actually, for the *Toxic Spew*, it was impressive that any kind of order had returned *at all.*

'Captain, we're going to have to think of something, and fast!' said Maxie at the flight controls. 'Otherwise we're going to get sucked so far into that black hole we won't be able to get out and we'll all die a terrible, agonising, and literally *long-drawn-out death*!'

'Captain I'm too young to die a terrible, agonising, and literally *long-drawn-out death*!'

sobbed Yargal, sticky grey snot splattering onto everyone within a tentacle's reach of her slimy slug-like body.

Harvey's mind raced. What on Earth could he do?

(I hate to be overly critical at a time like this, but it seems a bit of a daft question.

They weren't on Earth and when Harvey had been on Earth the only captain experience he'd had was with the Highford All Stars – and you get a lot of black holes on a football pitch, do you?)

Fighting back the panic, Harvey told himself to dig deep for an idea – *any* idea. The thing about the Highford All Stars is, they aren't all that good – but their captain is. They were bottom of the league until Harvey took over two seasons ago and now they're steadily working their way up the table. This is partly because Harvey is very good at reading a game but *mostly* because he has the guts to change tactics mid match.

Time to ditch the game plan

He's always telling his team that there's no point sticking to your game plan, or what you practised in training, if it isn't working on the pitch. And if you're playing a forward-attacking game and you're losing, then you have to stop and fall back on your defence.

That's it! thought Harvey, *stop and fall back!*

'Hit the brakes,' he yelled. 'And REVERSE. Maximum cosmic speed!'

Maxie yanked the supersonic brakes on and shoved the reversing rockets on to FULL. The engines screamed and juddered as 900,000 units of cosmic power (from two really, really big batteries) forced them to go backwards.

The crew held their breath as slowly, horribly slowly, agonisingly slowly in fact, the grotty little garbage ship gradually reversed out of the powerful pull of the black hole and to safety.

'YAHOO!'

The entire bridge crew erupted into wild cheering, except Yargal who cried with relief. It was disgusting.

'My hero!' she cried, slapping Harvey soggily on the back. He tried not to flinch.

Maxie gave him a huge grin from under her multi-coloured fringe.

'Oh, well done, sir,' cried Gizmo, coming over to shake his hand enthusiastically.

'Shall I stick the hydrosonic hyperdrive lever back on?' asked Scrummage, picking up the broken handle and some sticky tape. 'And we can have another go?'

'NO!' yelled everyone.

Maxie switched off the Anti-Pasta Intergalactic Shield 3000 and the force shield surrounding the ship disappeared.

(I say 'disappeared'. Actually it popped like a giant bubble, leaving greasy smears on the outside of the ship. But I wasn't

going to put that because it doesn't sound very hi-tech or space-like does it?)

Then Maxie plotted the new course taking the longer route to *Waitless*, on the 3D star map, showing Harvey as she did so. 'We'll take the Interstellar Scenic Highway Z98, nip past the Lesser Spotted Nebula, through the Greater Megon Belt, hang a left at these two planets, Caloris Major and Caloris Lite, bear right at the Moons of Dorus and then the intergalactic super store will be up ahead of us.'

It was quite a wiggly route, marked in bright purple and, worryingly, littered with exclamation mark signs.

'What are those?' asked Harvey warily.

'Tourist sites. It's the scenic route.' she explained. 'But it shouldn't be too bad. Unless we get stuck behind an enormous P&O cruise ship.'

'A "P&O" cruise ship?!' exclaimed Harvey, who was pretty sure his granny had been on one of those.

'Yes. Stands for 'Pangalactic and Orbital cruise ships,' said Maxie. 'They're massive. Some of the biggest crafts in outer space and horribly SLOOOOOW.' She ended in a groan.

Harvey grinned, then sat back in his captain's chair and braced himself for the gobsmackingly brilliant moment when the plucky little garbage ship careered forward at full cosmic speed.

ZZZZZIIIIIIP!

This time he hardly cracked his head at all on the back of his seat and there was only a small

THWACK!

CHAPTER ELEVEN

Interstellar Scenic Highway Z98

Maxie wasn't kidding – it really was the scenic route. Had Harvey and the crew not been so hungry they might have pulled over in a hyperspace lay-by to enjoy the view. It was stunning. But then most of the Entire Known Universe, and Beyond, is pretty awesome.

(It might be helpful to explain that the Lesser Spotted Nebula, and the mighty Greater Megon Belt are both major tourist attractions in Galaxy 43b. Parking can be a bit tricky at peak times.

To be honest, the two dwarf planets, Caloris Major and Caloris Lite, are a bit ordinary. I mean, once you've seen it raining diamonds, well you've seen it, haven't you? Oh, and by the way, the toilets there are a bit basic so I suggest you bring your own paper. And a disinfectant spray. And a really strong hand cleaner.

But the multiple Moons of Dorus are breathtaking and well worth a visit – well, that's if your tiny little planet ever figures out how to go a bit further than your very own little moon.

Honestly, you have no idea what you're missing.)

As the *Toxic Spew* meandered it's way along the Interstellar Scenic Highway Z98, heading for the intergalactic super store, *Waitless*, Harvey added 'new hydrosonic hyperdrive lever' to the shopping list. Not long after, he had to add 'roll of electrical wire' to the list as well. Gordon had wriggled his way into the engineering desk and treated himself to a good chew.

BZZZZZZ, DZZZZZ, CRACKLE!

went the desk as bare wires collided and sparks shot out from the controls, and

'AAAAARGH! OI! YEEOOWCH!'

went Gizmo as he ducked the sparks, grabbed Gordon and got a mega painful sting from his tail.

(It might interest you to know that a baby Gordonzola, despite being one of the adorably cutest, fubzy-wubzyist little aliens in the Entire Known Universe, and Beyond, has a sting in its tail that measures 13.4 megahurts on the Pangalactic Pain Scale.

But since you're not likely to ever meet one, maybe you don't care?

Gizmo does.)

Gizmo promptly dropped Gordon onto the deck with a yelp.

'Careful! You'll hurt him,' cried Scrummage dashing over to pick him up. 'It's not his fault – you scared him.'

'He's eating the wires!' erupted Gizmo.

'He's teething!' cried Scrummage protectively, cuddling the baby alien.

'Well, he can go and teethe somewhere else!' snapped Gizmo, nursing his throbbing hand.

Scrummage sat the Gordonzola on his lap. Blimey, it's a good job Gordon's small. Scrummage's belly sticks out so much there's hardly any lap left. Maxie looked at Harvey and rolled her eyes.

Another bad game plan

There were still a gazillion mega-miles to go to get to *Waitless* and even Harvey was struggling with hunger now. So he asked the computer if it had any games they could play.

'Games?!' cried the computer. 'Are you kidding? I am a galaxy-class 75b SpaceCorp computer with a CosmicCore processor and 215 megatronbyte boogle memory – of course I have *games*! I don't like to brag, but I'm programmed with the top ten all-time best-selling games in the Entire Known Universe, and Beyond. I'll just pick one at random.'

Excellent, thought Harvey and sat back in his seat expectantly.

'I spy with my little eye something beginning with S,' said the computer.

'Space,' chorused the rest of the crew wearily.

'How did you guess?' it cried.

'It's always space,' they moaned.

'That's not true!' huffed the computer. 'Sometimes it's G. G for . . .'

'Garbage,' they groaned.

'Or F. F for . . .'

'Filth,' they droned.

'Well, don't blame me,

a) I didn't choose the mission, and

b) you're bin men, so what did you expect?'

it finished and bleeped off in a sulk.

Waitless ahead!

Finally, hours and hours later, the crew, now almost fainting with hunger, neared the I.S.S. *Waitless*.

Harvey watched as the intergalactic super store loomed closer. It looked like a motorway service station but *inside* a massive snow globe shaker. (Without the snow, obviously. It doesn't snow in space.) In the centre of the complex, dozens of docking bays sat between a fuel station on one side, and a super store on the other. A giant see-through hangar covered it completely.

Scrummage crawled to the front vision screen and pressed his nose against it pathetically. 'Food!' he whimpered weakly, 'FOOD!'

Waitless
SUPA-STORE
Waitless

As they neared the enormous see-through hangar doors, Harvey suddenly panicked that they wouldn't open and the plucky little intergalactic garbage ship would slam into them, shattering the plasti-glass into thousands of tiny shards that would spiral off across the galaxy.

(Technically speaking, he needn't have worried. Plasti-glass is unbreakable so it would have been the Toxic Spew, not the hangar doors, that would have shattered into thousands of tiny shards and spiralled off across the galaxy.

Or, come to think of it, maybe he wasn't worrying enough?)

'Er, Maxie . . .' he said worriedly as the gap closed to about 100 metres and the doors still hadn't opened.

Maxie was busy setting the controls to STANDBY AUTO-PARK. 'Hang on a mo,' she said, not looking up.

'But Maxie!' he warned more urgently, as the gap closed to about 10 metres.

'MAXIE!' he screamed as the gap closed to 1 metre.

CHAPTER TWELVE

Waitless

Casually Maxie looked up just as, with less than 10 centimetres to go, the massive hangar doors shot open and the *Toxic Spew* slid inside. The doors immediately closed behind them, keeping as much air as possible inside the dome.

Harvey didn't actually see any of that happen – he'd clapped his hands over his eyes in terror. When he peered over his fingers, it was to see Maxie laughing at him from under her multi-coloured fringe.

'Fine captain you're turning out to be!' she

sniggered. 'Scared of a pair of auto-opening hyperspace hangar doors!'

Harvey grinned at her, and then laughed too. You didn't get to be picked captain of the Highford All Stars for two seasons running if you didn't know how to laugh at yourself.

Slowly the *Toxic Spew* descended towards the deck, Maxie using the ship's rear parking booster jets to slow them down and steer them towards the docking bays.

They were all empty.

'Pick a number!' said Maxie jokingly to Harvey. 'Any number you like!'

'Er . . . eight,' said Harvey, instinctively opting for his shirt number in the Highford All Stars.

Skilfully, Maxie parked the spaceship in docking bay number eight, slap bang in the centre of the parking lines.

'Food!' groaned Scrummage again, pitifully. 'So near and yet so far!'

Harvey peered out through the smeary vision screens that lined three sides of the bridge. The lights were on, but there were no other spaceships, and no one to be seen anywhere. *Waitless* was deserted.

'Is it usually this quiet?' he asked.

'Perhaps they're closed,' suggested Yargal.

'They never close,' announced Maxie.

Harvey didn't like it. He didn't like it at all. But with absolutely no food left on the ship, and a ravenous, mutinous crew, he didn't have any other options, ideas or excuses. There was no escaping it – they had to go shopping.

Scrummage wanted to take Gordon but Harvey told him to leave him on the ship with Snuffles.

'Snuffles, on guard!' ordered Harvey, and the hound proudly stood protectively over the little alien. 'I meant guard the ship, not Gordon!' sighed Harvey despairingly.

A painful drop

The crew headed down to the ship's exit pod. As the outer doors slid open they stood back politely to let Harvey go first. Well, he *thought* they were being polite. Actually they were letting him go first to make sure everything was all right.

Everything wasn't.

The instant Harvey stepped out of the ship, his feet lifted off the deck and he floated up!

'Woooaaaah!' he cried. 'HELP!'

Looking on the bright side, at least Harvey was *inside* an enormous plasti-glass domed hangar, and wasn't in danger of drifting off into the lonely depths of outer space, dying almost immediately from lack of air and never to be seen again. (Unless he floated near the doors and they opened automatically, of course, which would be a bit, er . . . dodgy. Well, fatal really.)

But anyhow, Harvey was too busy to worry about that – he was desperately scrabbling to snatch hold of a sticky-out bit of the ship. He missed.

'Harvey!' screamed Maxie jumping up and trying to grab him. She couldn't reach.

'Splattering upchuck!' cursed Scrummage.

'Captain! Come back!' cried Gizmo.

'How?'yelled Harvey.

Suddenly he felt a disgustingly soggy tentacle slap itself round his ankle. Yargal had grasped him. Her giant foot sucker held her firmly on to the deck and she hauled him to safety.

He never thought he'd be glad to feel Yargal's sloppy grey slime oozing through his sock and onto his bare flesh. But there you are.

'Why is the artificial gravity turned off?' demanded Gizmo.

'Who knows?' shrugged Yargal.

'Who cares!' replied Maxie.

'FOOD!' pleaded Scrummage.

Clinging on to anything they could – the docking bay barriers, advertising stands and mostly Yargal (which was about as easy as gripping a wet bar of soap, and about as pleasant as hugging a slug) they struggled to the shop.

Gizmo found the artificial gravity controls and switched the system back on.

THUD! THUMP! PLONK!

Everyone landed painfully on the deck. Scrummage stumbled to his feet and staggered into the shop.

Everywhere they looked they saw signs that the intergalactic super store had been abandoned in a hurry – dirty plates and cups lay dropped and deserted in the café area, loaded shopping trolleys left at the checkouts, and full shopping bags just dumped on the deck.

It was worryingly quiet.

It was also worryingly smelly.

Any other crew would have been wary – their highly trained senses and even more highly trained brains would have detected there was something very wrong.

But this was the crew of the *Toxic Spew* and

a) there was nothing highly trained about any of them, and
b) they were used to the disgusting smell

of the *Toxic Spew* (anything smelled better than that)

Plus

c) they were very, very hungry. Way too hungry to worry about anything except how quickly they could rip open food packets and cram the contents into their mouths.

(Seriously? After all their multiple intergalactic missions they're too worryingly stupid not guess that something that's worryingly quiet and worryingly smelly is . . . er . . . worryingly worrying?

Oh, good grief.)

CHAPTER THIRTEEN

Spookily quiet on the I.S.S.

Harvey and the crew could hear their space boots clunking on the metal deck and echoing all around them as they made their way to the shop. Spookily, Harvey had a horrible feeling they were being watched. Warning bells went off in his head.

(No, not literally. Don't be stupid! He's not a robot, for goodness' sake.)

The store was deserted – and trashed.

Some of the checkout tills had been left open,

and a digital voice kept repeating: 'Please take your bags . . . please take your bags . . . please take your bags . . .' It was incredibly irritating.

The freezer door was wide open and a large pool of water and melted ice cream had dribbled out and pooled onto the deck (possibly mint chocolate chip and raspberry cookie crumble, judging by the colour and texture. Unless it was vomit, of course.)

A shelf of Spaceghetti in Baked Stars Sauce had been tipped over and the cartons had burst all over the floor. Harvey noticed some weird-looking footprints in the puddle of sauce.

(Excuse me, but can I just remind you that Captain Harvey Drew is from a tiny little planet called Earth which no one in Galaxy 43b has even heard of? And that up until a few weeks ago, he'd never even left that tiny little planet in its remote corner of the universe?

So who's he to decide whether the footprints in the sauce look 'weird' or not?

SAVE!
!
38
39
43
42

I don't mean to be rude or anything. I'm just saying . . .)

In the café area, orange and lemon Spaceade drinks were spilled across the deck, tables lay knocked over and a half-eaten Cosmic Cream Cheese Custard and Crackling Cake sat abandoned on a plate. Scrummage scooped it up hungrily and shoved it in his mouth.

'Yummy!' he spluttered excitedly, spitting custard and cake crumbs everywhere.

Maxie grabbed a half-empty pack of Space Radar Crisps, poured them into her mouth and munched furiously. Gizmo, finding that some coins had been left in the *Any Food in the Universe* vending machine, used it all up to buy a Super Delux Starspresso drink, a Comet Curry and Cabbage Soufflé with Red Custard.

Harvey headed off to the grocery section. It's not that he's fussy. Just that he has more self control.

Spookily quiet on the *Toxic Spew*

Meanwhile, back on the bridge of the *Toxic Spew*, it was spookily quiet too. Eventually, even the computer noticed.

'Hello?' it said, suspiciously. 'Is there anyone there?'

There was no reply.

WHIRR, SZCHHHH, WHIRR

went the computer's CCTV camera as it scanned the entire ship.

It searched the command bridge,
the galley and sickbay,
the crew's quarters,
all the corridors,
the garbage hold and finally, as a last resort,
the toilets.

(And believe me, looking into the toilets on the *Toxic Spew* was absolutely a last resort.)

'Hello? Coo-eeee! HELLOO-OOO!' it called.

But the *Toxic Spew* was deserted.

'Huh! Typical!' it snorted huffily. 'Don't bother to tell me you're going out will you? I mean you could have left a note! Just feel free to abandon me here, all alone and deserted, with no one except a stupid Hazard Hunting Hound and a dumb baby Gordonzola on the bridge for company!'

At that point the computer noticed what the dumb baby Gordonzola was happily doing on the bridge.

'No, Gordon. NO!' cried the computer in a shocked tone. 'Don't do that on the bridge! Bad Gordon. Bad baby Gordonzola!'

But Gordon ignored it and carried on doing whatever it was he was doing, until he'd finished. Snuffles put his paws over his eyes in embarrassment.

'Oh good grief,' exclaimed the computer in disgust, and bleeped off in despair.

CHAPTER FOURTEEN

All-out feeding frenzy

By now the rest of the crew had joined Harvey in the food department and had immediately launched into an all-out feeding frenzy. It was gross. Astonishingly gross.

(Can I just say that the scene was so revolting I don't even want to describe it? You're going to have to make do with your own imagination and these sound effects.

Believe me, I'm doing you a favour.)

RIP!

TEAR!

SCRUNCH!

MUNCH, CRUNCH!

CHOMP, CHEW!

GUZZLE, GUZZLE, GULP!

BURB . . . BELCH . . . BUUUURP!

Harvey, however, was too gobsmacked looking at the food on sale to notice the disgusting table manners of his crew.

He gazed at the 'Outer Space Fruit and Veg' display in astonishment. There were dark orange Supersonic Sprouts, something called 'Sprocolli' (which looks like a cross between a cauliflower and a head of broccoli and a bright pink brain and tastes astonishingly scrummy – especially the stalks), bags of Mixed AstroNuts, and a heap of Bouncing Bananas, which were an alarmingly bright blue.

Harvey couldn't resist trying a bouncing banana. He pulled one off the pile.

(No, not to eat, he just wanted to see if it would bounce.) He chucked it onto the floor . . . hard. It did.

'Whoah!' cried Harvey ducking, as the bright blue fruit hit the deck and bounced crazily around like a demented powerball.

BO-IIIIING! BO-IIIIING!

BO-IIIIING! *BO-IIIIING!*

BO-IIIIING! B-B-B-B-B-BOING.

Harvey finally caught the bounding banana, and put it back. Then he wandered over and scanned the breakfast food shelves. They were stacked with boxes of Astroid Pops, Spaceflakes and packs of Multi-Coloured JellyBread Rolls.

He ripped open a packet of Astroid Pops and peered at the contents. It looked like ordinary cereal, so he grabbed a handful and shoved it in his mouth.

It was AWESOME!!!

POP! POPAPOP! POP!

As soon as the cereal puffs hit his tongue they exploded like popcorn, flooding his mouth with the taste of salted caramel, white chocolate, sticky toffee pudding and raspberry sauce. Merrily munching his way down the box he moved along to a section labelled SupaCosmicSupaSpeediSuppers. It was full of tins of Space Noodle Spolognaise with Meateor Balls, Asteroid Risotto with Orbital Onion Gravy and Purple Pasta Planets with 100% Blue Cheese Moon Balls.

'Blue Cheese Moon Balls? Is that a joke?' he asked, turning to the crew, who were still scoffing.

'No,' said Yargal, between gooey mouthfuls of a pink iced strawberry jam and mackerel doughnut. 'The Moons of Margherita are made of blue cheese. Don't you get cheese from your moon?'

'Er, no,' said Harvey witheringly, thinking that Yargal was winding him up. 'We make cheese from milk.'

Yargal quivered like a jelly and snorted with laughter. (Well, technically she snotted with laughter – from both nostrils. Yuk.) 'Now *that's* a good joke!'

Harvey gave up.

Harvey sticks to his guns

After everyone had almost stuffed themselves sick, Harvey, Yargal and Scrummage started loading several trolleys with food while Gizmo and Maxie went off to the hypersonic tools section to find a new hydrosonic hyperdrive lever and a roll of electrical wire. Gizmo grabbed a whole stack of snazzy spare parts and bits of kit and caboodle for the *Toxic Spew* and put them in a trolley too. He had no idea what any of it was – but it all looked 'state of the galaxy' cool.

Looking at the heaps of food and piles of equipment, Harvey asked how they were going to pay for everything. Everyone looked at everyone else and then shrugged. None of them had any space cash – they'd all been hoping he had.

He hadn't.

'Who cares?' argued Scrummage. 'There's no one here. We can just do a runner!'

'We can't do that!' cried Harvey.

'Of course we can't!' agreed Gizmo. 'The security alarms will go off!'

'Not if we rip the tags off,' said Maxie, instantly tearing the labels off everything in her trolley.

'No,' said Harvey pointedly. 'We can't do it *because it's theft*.'

'So?' asked Scrummage.

Three pairs of turquoise eyes and three googly ones on stalks stared at Harvey blankly.

Harvey took a deep breath and tried to keep calm. 'Stealing is wrong,' he explained patiently.

'Who cares?' shrugged Maxie.

'I do!' spluttered Harvey, and he insisted that if they couldn't pay, then they should collect the garbage to make up for it and do some tidying up too. The crew groaned, complained bitterly and whinged spectacularly. But Harvey stuck to his guns.

So they all pitched in to clear up the worst of the mess and then Gizmo and Maxie went back to the *Toxic Spew* in the docking bay to fill up with fuel and give the ship a basic service to try to make it space-worthy. (Huh! Fat chance.) And Yargal carried on piling food into trolleys, while Harvey and Scrummage set off for the garbage control area. Harvey reminded everyone to be careful and keep a sharp lookout.

Something wasn't right – he just knew it.

(But then, Harvey doesn't have a lot of experience as a spaceship captain, so he might be wrong.

On the other hand, he might not be.)

CHAPTER FIFTEEN

Servicing and supplies

Back outside the ship, Gizmo undid the intergalactic fuel cap and filled the *Toxic Spew*'s fuel tank up with the Megatron 500 Insta-Refueller pump.

(Oh hang on, I've just remembered – you have absolutely no idea what type of fuel goes in a spaceship do you? You probably think it's something like the sort of petrol you use for those funny little cars you like to travel around in on your planet.

Oh, please.

Most of the spaceships in Galaxy 43b use Three Star Premium GasoLime. This is a supercharged green gloppy goo that looks and smells very much like lime jelly. Whatever you do, don't muddle the two up. Partly because spaceships don't run at all well on lime jelly, but mostly because Three Star Premium GasoLime tastes terrible with ice cream – and even worse with peanut butter.)

Maxie was busily using the GalacticAirHose to pump up the front bumper, but there was a big puncture in the inner tube, so it didn't work.

Then she tried cleaning the front vision screen with the Scrub-O-Matic spray. But the space-dirt was so thick that that didn't work either.

So she tried mending the broken landing gear with a pair of super hydronic elastic braces. Guess what? That didn't work either.

Finally, she tested the brakes and lights.

They didn't work either, of course, but then she knew that already.

* * *

Meanwhile, Gizmo had gone back onto the command bridge on the *Toxic Spew* to fix the wiring on the engineering controls, and replace the hypersonic hyperdrive lever on the flight desk. As soon as the bridge doors schwoooshed open, he gasped and reeled backwards in horror! There were puddles of Gordonzola wee *everywhere*!

'GORDON!!!' he bellowed furiously.

Tempting goodies!

Meanwhile, back in the grocery department of *Waitless*, Yargal had just about finished loading trolleys and was now struggling to wheel all six of them (one in each tentacle) along at the same time. They just wouldn't go in a straight line and kept crashing into each other. It didn't help that all of them were ridiculously overladen, so every time they bumped into anything, piles of packages slithered off.

But it was made much, much harder by the fact that Yargal was constantly tempted by lots of other goodies and treats and kept letting go of one trolley to add something to another one.

'Oooooh. I must have some of those!' she said, reaching out a slimy tentacle for some Hovering Fizzy Saucers and Gooey Galactic Gummies.

CRASH . . . BASH!

'Ooops!' she cried gaily, as one of the trolleys smashed into the side of the walkway and nearly tipped over, scattering groceries everywhere. Yargal just sighed happily and stacked it all up again.

Ominous noises from the garbage bin

In the garbage control room Harvey was more and more sure that something was very wrong.

The funny smell was getting stronger. He wished Snuffles was with him because the huge Hazard Hunting Hound was

a) good at hunting hazards, and
b) huge, and
c) not to mention the owner of more teeth than a fully grown Great White Shark with a good dentist.

Scrummage was also worried. Very worried. But he didn't want to show it. Not because he's brave, but because he's reckless.

I mean, think about it – just because you're *pretending* everything is all right, doesn't mean everything actually *is* all right and sometimes, usually in fact, it's probably a good idea to mention that it *isn't*. All right, that is. Or not. Or something.

(Sorry, I think I might have confused you a bit there. I certainly confused myself.)

Hurriedly, Scrummage set the garbage controls to AutoSpew and it was about that moment that he and Harvey noticed some ominous noises coming from the industrial-sized rubbish tank in the middle of the room.

'Flickering spew!' muttered Scrummage nervously under his breath.

'Is it supposed to be doing that?' asked Harvey.

'It's probably nothing to worry about. Let's just get back to the ship,' said Scrummage carelessly, too carelessly, before he scarpered – *at full pelt*. Harvey sprinted after him. If there was something dodgy or, more probably, downright deadly dangerous in the garbage room he wasn't going to stick around to find out what. Not because he's a wimp but because he's not stupid.

Yargal had finally managed to get to the exit with her multiple trolleys. Humming a cheerful Yargillian tune merrily to herself, she rounded them up, got them all going in the same direction and pushed through the doors . . . Instantly every alarm in the entire intergalactic service station went off.

WHOOP! WHOOP! WHOOP!

She hadn't thought to take the security labels off.

Alarms screamed – and so did Yargal. 'Aaaaaaaargh!'

Then suddenly . . .

and terrifyingly . . .

CHAPTER SIXTEEN

SuperStain and SuperSting

Three *enormous* security drones zoomed up from out of nowhere, zapping their Stop'n'Spray SuperStain Paintballs at anything and anyone that moved. Which, just at that moment, happened to be Yargal and her trolleys and Maxie at the service docking bay.

ZAP! ZAP! ZAP-ZAP!

They might be called SuperStain Paintballs, but SuperSting Pain-Balls is probably a better name for them.

SAVE!

SPLAT!

'YEEEOWCH!' Maxie yelped as a yellow pellet thwacked her in the leg! She gave up trying to service the ship and made a dive for the ship's exit pod and the safety of the *Toxic Spew*.

SPLAT! SPLAT! SPLATTER, SPLAT!

'OUCH! OWWW!' wailed Yargal as an orange paintball walloped onto her soft green body, quickly followed by a candyfloss-pink one, and two pale blue ones.

(I'm sorry to butt in at this thrilling moment, but I have an important information announcement for you.

I know it's not likely, but if you do go to an intergalactic super store anywhere in Galaxy 43b – don't do anything to upset the security drones.

Because not only do they have six

extra-long extending arms – each ending in a powerful metal claw, but two of those claws have guns, and two hold handcuffs. And you don't have to be a maths genius to know that that leaves two claws spare for grabbing hold of you. Painfully hard.

They whizz around incredibly fast on a single wheel. A blindingly bright red light flashes furiously on top of their cube-shaped heads. They have laser eyes with supersonic sight and X-ray glasses. (Which actually makes them look mega cool.)

They are also ENORMOUS. At least 9 feet 7 inches tall. It's almost impossible to escape them.

They come in three colours. Red, blue and green – which is all very pretty, but frankly who cares? Because if you're close enough to see what colour they are, you're close enough to be in terrible trouble – and even more pain.)

Ducking madly and swatting wildly at the volley of paintballs, Yargal grabbed the first missiles she could reach from the nearest trolley and hurled them at the droids with all her might, letting rip with all six tentacles at once.

'Take that!' she cried furiously, hurling half a dozen bright blue bananas at them.

But the flying fruits just bounced straight off the metal droids without even leaving a dent or a nasty blue graze.

BOING!

BOING!

BOINGaBOING!

BOING!

ZAP! ZAP-ZAP!

'OW, OUCH!' squealed Yargal as the droids carried on firing mercilessly at her. Dragging her trolleys along with her as she went, she raced to the ship as fast as she could. In other words, very slowly.

KER-SPLAT!

'OWWWW!!!!'

Actually, make that agonisingly slowly.

Fluttering upchuck!

Harvey and Scrummage arrived at the entrance just in time to see Yargal slither up to the exit pod of the *Toxic Spew* with three enormous security droids taking pot shots at her. Hurriedly she hurled the shopping inside and then grasping the doorway with all six tentacles, she hauled her quivering slimy body in afterwards.

'Fluttering upchuck!' yelled Scrummage.

Which wasn't wise. Because up until that moment, the droids hadn't noticed Harvey and Scrummage, but now, to their horror, the security droids turned their supersonic laser eyes directly on to them and trundled towards them – menacingly.

(You know, in that ominous, threatening, robotic way that only robots can really do well.

Except of course you don't know, do you? Because you've hardly invented any droids in your distant corner of the universe, have you?

Honestly, it's a lot less tricky than you think. I mean obviously, it's harder than making the perfect pepperoni, pineapple and parsnip pizza with a three chilli cheese and marmalade chutney crust stuffing, but it's much easier than rocket science.)

'What are we going to do?' wailed Scrummage, as the enormous droids zoomed towards them.

Harvey thought about making a run for it. But his Rubbish Officer was a much slower runner – and a much bigger target. And you didn't leave your teammate . . . er crew member, exposed like that.

But then Scrummage had a brilliant idea. He radioed the *Toxic Spew*: 'Gizmo! The security droids are metal. You can use the Magno Beam to capture them!'

It was a brilliant plan. Except that Gizmo didn't know how. In fact, only Scrummage knew how to operate the Magno Beam – or any of the garbage collection devices on the *Toxic Spew*. And let's face it, this was hardly the time for Scrummage to stop everything and give Gizmo a basic step-by-step lesson.

Well, not with three enormous security droids bearing down on them, it wasn't.

Then Harvey had another, equally brilliant idea.

'Scrummage, grab hold of something!' he ordered and grasping the artificial gravity lever he yanked it to 'OFF'!

It was a brilliant plan. Except security droid wheels are magnetic so the robots stayed firmly on the deck while Harvey's and Scrummage's legs floated upwards until they were floating upside down, the blood rushing to their heads. Harvey promptly yanked the gravity control back to 'ON'.

But by now, one of the droids (the blue one, actually) was dangerously close.

'RUN!' yelped Scrummage, sprinting off, leaving Harvey to race after him.

Fat chance. Within seconds they'd both been grabbed in the robot's powerful claws.

'AAAAAARGH!' they screamed as the droid zoomed off across the deck with its metal extending arms wrapped firmly round them!

Clamped in the painfully tight grip of the merciless machine, Harvey's mind raced frantically.

Scrummage's mind, on the other hand, and under the other arm, *panicked* frantically. 'Waaaaah!' he shrieked.

Suddenly, to his utter horror, Harvey realised they were heading for the *Toxic Spew* – and Yargal hadn't closed the exit pod! The entire ship and crew would be at risk if the robot got onto the ship. He had to get the crew to shut the door! He struggled to reach his radio – but his arms were held in a vice-like grip. He couldn't move.

'Scrummage!' Harvey yelled desperately. 'Can you reach your radio?'

'Waaaaaaaah!' continued Scrummage.

Harvey took that as a 'No'.

Outclassed and outpaced

As a football captain, Harvey always says 'the game isn't over until it's over'. Even if you're six goals down at half-time, outclassed and outpaced, you don't give up. So Harvey went for a change of tactics, and started wriggling wildly and violently kicking his legs. He was determined to get free and protect his crew!

(For the record – can I just say how amazed and impressed I am by Harvey's courage and doggedness?

No, seriously. If I had to choose one word to describe him right now it would be:

Heroic.

Or Valiant.

Or Fearless.

Or maybe Bold?

Or . . . oh, I dunno . . . you pick one.)

But the robot only tightened its grip and raced up to the *Toxic Spew!* Flinging Harvey and Scrummage roughly in through the exit pod, the droid hauled itself up after them. Then, to their astonishment, it slammed the door behind them all!

'Save me!' it begged, in a metallic, rusty voice.

Harvey and Gizmo stared at it open-mouthed, way too stunned to speak.

'I'm not a security droid! I'm a NerdBot 1000! I was sent here by mistake!' explained the robot. 'My programmed functions are: cleaning, tidying and making galaxy-class galactic coffee – with soft brown sugar, cream and *caramel topping*. Not chasing, handcuffing and shooting shoplifters! I did try to tell the manager,' it complained miserably, 'but honestly, you humanoids are all the same. You think that just because we robots all look the same we *are* all the same. Take me with you!' it rasped, clasping its claws together pleadingly.

Harvey made an instant, but brilliant command decision. Partly because the NerdBot 1000 had just rescued them from a horrible fate, but *mostly* because the *Toxic Spew* seriously, desperately and urgently needed a cleaner. He said: 'Fine by me!'

Then he sprinted to the bridge, with Scrummage and the droid following.

Don't panic!

SCHWOOOOSH

The bridge doors opened and Harvey raced through. He was relieved to see Maxie and Yargal were safe. Oddly rainbow-coloured, but safe. They looked liked they'd survived an explosion in the decorating department of a DIY store.

Peering through the grimy, paint-splattered vision screens round the three sides of the bridge, the crew watched the other two security droids trundling away. They'd clearly lost interest now that the crew were safely locked inside the *Toxic Spew*.

A few moments later Scrummage and the NerdBot 1000 arrived on the bridge.

'Aaaaaargh!' panicked Yargal, waggling her tentacles hysterically. Gizmo gulped and scrambled under his seat.

'Harvey, look out!' yelled Maxie, leaping clean over the flight desk and ducking down behind it.

'Don't panic!' cried Harvey. 'It's OK! This is er . . . a NerdBot and um . . .' Harvey suddenly realised he didn't know whether a NerdBot was a 'he' or a 'she' so he said, 'and, it's joining the crew!'

'What?' demanded Maxie promptly standing up and glaring at him challengingly from under her fringe.

'Captain!' exclaimed Gizmo pompously (well, as pompously as he could since he was scrabbling out from under his chair at the time). 'You can't go around taking on crew members without even consulting us.'

'Yes he can, he's the captain,' retorted Maxie, clambering back over the flight desk.

'I'm Nerdie,' creaked the robot, rumbling forward. Then it stopped and scanned the bridge with its supersonic laser eyes and the entire crew winced with embarrassment. As usual, the bridge was utterly gross and even worse, splattered with puddles of Gordon's wee.

'It's filthy!' croaked Nerdie rustily, and using one claw to detach its VoltaVacuum attachment, and the others to produce a mop and bucket, a dustpan and brush and a bin liner, it started cleaning up.

The crew were gobsmacked. If you'd slapped them round face with a damp duster and a soggy squeezy mop they couldn't have been more surprised. Not even if you'd followed that by bashing them with the bucket.

'Good luck with that!' snorted Maxie to Nerdie, sarcastically.

'Oh good decision, sir!' exclaimed Gizmo.

Scrummage pretended to vomit in disgust at the sight of Gizmo creeping up to Harvey.

Yargal scooped up Gordon. 'You need a nappy!' she announced and slurped off to the galley to make one out of some kitchen roll and goo-proof plasters.

Big mistake

Then, much to the bridge crew's annoyance, Harvey insisted they finish collecting the garbage from *Waitless*. Which, as a matter of fact, was all very noble of him, but turned out to be a big mistake.

(If you're one of those readers who hates

being given hints like that and you want to know why it was a big mistake, then you can turn to page 146 and find out.

But then you'd skip pages 130 to 145 wouldn't you, and you might miss something important, mightn't you?

Of course you might not.

I'm not telling.)

Sighing meaningfully and rolling her eyes pointedly, Maxie positioned the *Toxic Spew* near the garbage exit pipe of the intergalactic super store. Then, muttering mightily and darkly, Scrummage hurriedly placed the Ultrawave 3.2 Vacuum Pump over the garbage outlet and set the controls to Super Nova Nozzle Plus. And very quickly, the rubbish was sucked into the pump bin in the hold and Scrummage detached the pipe.

'Now can we go?' said Maxie rudely, her hands poised impatiently over the flight controls. Harvey nodded and the Pilot Officer expertly flew the ship off the deck, out of the giant hangar doors of the intergalactic super store, and away into space.

But three seconds later

WHOOP! WHOOP! WHOOP!

all the alarms on the garbage control desk went off. Again.

CHAPTER SEVENTEEN

Three kinds of danger

'Now what's happened?' asked Harvey anxiously as Scrummage shot to his feet.

'Nothing to worry about!' replied Scrummage lightly, but he rushed off the command bridge with *alarming* and *suspicious* speed.

'I'll come with you!' called Harvey, jumping out of the captain's chair.

'No need sir, it's all under control,' lied the Rubbish Officer through his teeth and pelting off, the doors schwoooshing shut behind him.

'Can I offer you a cup of coffee, Captain?' rasped Nerdie, whirring up to him so Harvey might hear him over the deafening whooping.

'Not now, Nerdie,' said Harvey, giving the robot a withering look, which was of course, completely wasted on the droid, before ordering the computer to cut the alarms on the bridge.

Scrummage hurtled down to the Vacuum Control Centre in the ship's hold to check that his sticky-tape repair to the hosepipe was working.

It wasn't.

Steam poured out of the pump and the pressure dials read:

DANGER!

SERIOUS DANGER!

and

EXTREME DANGER!

'Fluttering puke!' he groaned, frantically strapping more tape around the hose.

'Bridge to Scrummage,' radioed Harvey, worriedly. 'Is everything all right down there?'

'Um . . .' replied Scrummage, trying to untangle a length of sticky tape from his fingers. Then, not wanting to fess up to Harvey that everything was *absolutely and completely and totally* NOT all right, he added: 'I'm just a bit tied up right now, Captain.'

So, back on the bridge, Harvey asked the computer for an update instead.

The computer's lights flashed on and off importantly for a few moments, then it said confidently: 'Well Captain, I don't like to worry you, but

a) there's a nasty crack in the subcarrier overlay cover of the nanodrive belt, and
b) three of the flange brackets have snapped right off, and
c) there's a bit of sticky toffee pudding trapped in the hyper-vacuum nodes,

which is causing a bit of a system breakdown . . . failure . . . meltdown . . . thing.'

'Are you making this up?' asked Harvey.

'Yes,' admitted the computer. 'I've absolutely no idea what's going on down there.'

Don't even ask, just run!

In the pump room Scrummage, on the other hand, was horribly aware of what was going on. The pressure dials now read:

INCREDIBLE DANGER!

UNIMAGINABLE DANGER!

and

DON'T EVEN ASK, JUST RUN!

Bravely (or possibly gobsmackingly stupidly), Scrummage ignored the flashing lights and shrieking alarms and was just tearing off another bit of sticky tape when

KA-BOOM-SPLAT!

The vacuum bin exploded.

It was so loud they could hear the explosion on the bridge.

'Scrummage?' called Harvey through the radio. 'SCRUMMAGE!'

There was no reply.

Harvey tore off the bridge, closely followed by Snuffles.

When they reached the Vacuum Control Centre, Harvey was hit by an appalling smell. It was like rotten eggs, mouldy blue cheese and soggy cabbage. Gagging badly, Harvey doubled over, trying not to throw up, while the Hazard Hunting Hound went bananas.

(If you've been following the story properly, you might be wondering whether he went bananas like your yellow Earth ones or like the bouncy blue outer space ones.

For the record – he did a lot of bouncing, but didn't go blue.

And can I just ask you something? Since, your Earth bananas just lie there doing nothing more interesting than going from yellow to black with a brown spotty phase in between, why do Earth people say someone 'went bananas' when you mean 'went crazy'?

Now that is crazy, if you ask me.)

GRRRR, WOUFF, WOUFF!

ARROUUUU!

went Snuffles, barking excitedly and bouncing about.

The stench made Harvey's eyes water so much he could hardly see. But through the plasti-glass window he could just about make out the crumpled form of Scrummage collapsed and coughing on the deck. A decidedly unhealthy looking thick yellow fog curled around the room.

'SCRUMMAGE!' he yelled. There was no response.

Harvey had no idea what the sickly smog was, but he knew he had to get Scrummage out – and supanova fast!

CHAPTER EIGHTEEN

A matter of life and death

Covering his nose and mouth with one hand, Harvey grabbed the door to the Vacuum Control Centre with the other and gave it a shove – but it was locked! He tried rattling it, kicking it and then taking a running jump at it (literally). Which was very dramatic but only ended up with him smashing his shoulder and bruising his knee. It wouldn't budge. And worse, he suddenly realised he couldn't contact the bridge, because the intercom was in the pump room!

Harvey raced back up to the bridge, his heart

thumping and his legs pounding. Luckily for Scrummage, Harvey was match fit.

Panting heavily, Harvey burst onto the bridge.

'Would you like that cup of coffee now, Captain?' croaked Nerdie hopefully.

'Not now, Nerdie!' gasped Harvey and, taking a deep breath, garbled: 'Scrummage-is-trapped-inside-the-Vacuum-Control-Centre-and-it's-full-of-yellow-smoke-and-I-think-it's-probably-poisonous-but-I-can't-open-the-doors!'

'Ah, yes, that'll be the automatic computerised safety lock,' nodded Gizmo, casually from the engineering desk.

'Well, turn it off and unlock the doors!' cried Harvey.

'I am sorry, Captain, but I'm afraid you're going to have to ask the computer if it will be so kind as to do that,' said Gizmo, carelessly.

Maxie rolled her eyes. 'Seriously Gizmo, is this the right moment for you to be hopeless as well as useless?' she said.

'Care for a coffee, Maxie?' asked Nerdie.

'Not now, Nerdie!' she snapped.

'Computer! Unlock the doors to the Vacuum Control Room!' ordered Harvey.

'Did I hear a *please*?' replied the computer snippily, it's lights blinking on and off crossly.

'No, you didn't! It's a matter of life and death!' yelled Harvey.

'It may very well be, but that's no reason to forget our manners, is it? And anyhow, I'm not sure it's such a good idea because

a) there might be something noxious in there that would poison the crew, or
b) there might be something toxic in there that would melt the ship, or
c) both.'

'I don't care!' bellowed Harvey. 'Now unlock those doors or Scrummage could die!'

'Hmmm, is that *really* a problem?' asked the computer with a gobsmacking lack of concern.

'No,' said Gizmo.

'YES!' yelled Harvey.

'Captain,' said Gizmo pompously. 'May I remind you of the Intergalactic Travel and Transport Pact rules and regulations regarding . . .'

'No!' barked Harvey, 'you may not!'

EVERYBODY PANIC!

'Gizmo can turn off the lock,' said Maxie suddenly.

'Can I?' asked Gizmo, spinning round to look at her. He was genuinely surprised.

'Yes. You can override the computer's locking system. Just hit the EVERYBODY PANIC! button.'

Gizmo scanned his engineering desk. 'Seriously! Who knew? Which one is that?'

'I'm taking a wild guess here, but maybe it's the big red button that says EVERYBODY PANIC! on it,' said Maxie, drily.

Gizmo punched it. 'How did you even know that?' he asked Maxie, very impressed.

Harvey didn't wait to hear the answer. He charged back off the bridge.

'I'm coming with you,' yelled Maxie, jumping up from the flight desk.

'No,' shouted Harvey. 'Stay here.'

'Why, because I'm a girl and you don't think I can cope with a little bit of poisonous gas that might melt my fingers to the bone, boil my eyeballs, rot my guts and slowly but surely choke me to death?' she snapped, pushing her sleeves up angrily and striding up to him.

No, ditzoid, because you're the only one who can fly the ship! But tell Yargal to get down there. Urgently.'

Maxie stopped in her tracks. 'Fair point. OK, fine. But don't call me ditzoid!' she hollered after him, as Harvey raced down to rescue Scrummage.

'Can I interest you in a cup of coffee, Gizmo?' creaked Nerdie brightly, as meanwhile the vast front vision screen was filled with a message that flashed on and off and read:

EVERYBODY PANIC!

EVERYBODY PANIC!

EVERYBODY PANIC!

It wasn't having much effect on anyone on the bridge of the *Toxic Spew.* Maxie ignored it, Nerdie was making coffee, Gizmo was too busy deciding how many sugars he wanted and, as usual, the computer couldn't be bothered.

Down in the ship's hold, Harvey raced along the filthy corridor to the Vacuum Control Centre and flung himself at the doors. They flew open. Which, on the one hand, was good for Scrummage, but on the other hand, was going to be very bad for Harvey and on the other, other hand (sorry, I've lost count of the hands, I think it's three so far), would be almost completely and utterly and totally *disastrous* for the *Toxic Spew* and the entire crew!

(Again, if you're one of those impatient readers who want skip forward to find out why, you'll have to flick to page . . .

Actually, no, I'm not telling you. It's only 7 pages. No sneaky peeking. You'll have to hang on, like everyone else.)

CHAPTER NINETEEN

Junk Skunks!

A dozen or so weird little aliens suddenly shot past Harvey and darted off down the corridor like lightning, their feet skittering on the metal deck.

Fat and rubbery, green and purple with lurid pink spots, Harvey thought they looked a bit like a cross between a speckled skunk, a toy frog and . . . a balloon. Some were much fatter than others, but they all looked like they'd been pumped full of air.

The stink was indescribable. It was so strong Harvey could literally feel it clawing up his

nose, clogging his throat and crawling into his lungs. It was so strong he could almost smell it with his ears.

Snuffles went berserk, snapping at the little aliens with his ferocious teeth, trying to catch them, but they were far too quick.

GRRR, SNAP! SNAP!

(I was tempted to interrupt the story here to give you some interesting facts about these little aliens. But then I decided to put them on a later page instead.

And, no, I'm not giving you the page number.

I know what you're like.)

Medical Officer Yargal had picked up her first aid kit and was hurriedly making her way down to the Vacuum Control Centre from the ship's sickbay as fast as her single, slimy foot would let her.

'Don't panic, Captain. I'm on my way!' she cried, frankly pointlessly because

a) there was no way he could hear her from where he was, and
b) in a life or death situation, the thought of a medical emergency being in the hands of a Yargillian is enough to make anybody panic.

SLITHER, SLITHER, SLIME . . . SLIDE.

She was going faster than a slug on a wet slope – going uphill.

It was quite impressive.

But not as impressive as the steaming cup of galaxy-class intergalactic coffee with two sugars, a whirl of cream and a snazzy zigzag of caramel cream sauce on the top which Nerdie was handing Gizmo on the command bridge.

In all his intergalactic missions Gizmo had never seen one quite like it. And neither had

Maxie who instantly demanded one like it but with chocolate sprinkles on top.

It's too late for me, Captain, but save yourself!

Meanwhile, back outside the Vacuum Control Centre, the strange little alien creatures bumped and bounced from one thing to another, and ducking and weaving they shot along the corridor. Now and then they'd stop, suck in their sides like a shrinking balloon, lift their tails and squirt out a bright green goo. Then, and this is the best bit, they'd turn and sniff the air – *proudly*.

Frankly, it was eye-wateringly ghastly.

Not that Harvey had time to hang about and watch them, or to notice the wafts of yellow smog drifting up from the dollops of goo on the deck and walls. He was too busy trying to rescue his Chief Rubbish Officer.

'Hold on, Scrummage,' he cried, grabbing

the outsized officer under the arms.

Coughing and choking, Scrummage clutched at Harvey's arm and managed to gasp: 'Junk Skunks! It's too late for me, Captain, but save yourself!' before he passed out completely.

Desperately, Harvey tried to haul Scrummage out of the fog-filled room. But it was hopeless. Obviously.

(Look, it's not going to take a genius with a calculator and a 'Power to Weight Ratio' App to know there was no way Harvey was going to be able to drag Scrummage even a nano-smidge across the floor.

I mean, you do the sums:

If Harvey (Life Form 1) weighs (x) and Scrummage (Life Form 2) weighs 3 × (x)

Then the chance of (Life Form 1) pulling (Life Form 2) = Fat Chance.)

But in any case, within seconds the appalling

reek had overpowered Harvey too! He blacked out and

THUD!

slumped onto the deck.

Whimpering anxiously, Snuffles darted over to Harvey and licked his face. Harvey didn't move. So Snuffles dribbled on him, nudged him with his huge meatball of a nose and scrabbled at him with his great hairy front paws – but he couldn't wake him up.

WHINE . . . WHIMPER, WHIMPER!

went Snuffles worriedly.

(Believe me, if being mauled and slobbered on by a fully grown Hazard Hunting Hound from Canine Major doesn't wake you up, you are seriously out cold.)

Giving up, Snuffles plonked his huge hairy hindquarters on the deck and howled like a heartbroken wolf.

AROOOO, AROUOUOU, AROOO!

CHAPTER TWENTY

The top ten most deadly garbage pests in the Entire Known Universe, and Beyond

THWACK SPLAT, THWACK SPLAT!

Harvey woke to find Yargal slapping him soggily across the face with her slimy tentacles. Yuk!

THWACK SPLAT!

'YEOWCH! OK, OK, STOP! I'm awake!' cried Harvey, hurriedly struggling to his feet.

Quickly he told Yargal about the invasion of Junk Skunks.

The Medical Officer gasped and one of her tentacles flew to her mouth in terror!

'They're in the top ten most dangerous garbage pests in the Entire Known Universe, and Beyond!' she shuddered, going a very pale green.

(She's right, they are.

They're at number four. If this is the sort of thing that interests you, then you can find a list of the top ten most deadly garbage pests in the Entire Known Universe, and Beyond, in the manual at the back of the book.

No, not now!

We're in the middle of a story, for crying out loud.)

'We'll have to get Scrummage to sickbay immediately!' exclaimed Yargal, wrapping two of her tentacles under his arms and trying to pick him up. No chance.

Harvey tried taking the legs end, and they both tried. But again, no chance.

In the end Harvey had to radio Nerdie to come and help. He warned Gizmo and Maxie that there was a pack of Junk Skunks loose on the ship at the same time.

'Stay on the bridge,' he ordered. 'And see if you can lock the doors.'

Lock the doors!

It won't surprise you to know that

a) Gizmo instantly assumed command of the command bridge, and
b) promptly blamed Harvey.

'If he hadn't *insisted* on collecting the garbage from the I.S.S. we wouldn't have vacuumed them onto the ship in the first place,' he sniffed scornfully.

'Yes, it's all his fault,' agreed the computer.

'The Junk Skunks were clearly the reason why *Waitless* was abandoned,' added Gizmo.

'He's a hopeless captain if you ask me,' said the computer.

'No, he's not, and we *didn't* ask you,' snapped Maxie. Her bright turquoise eyes glittered dangerously.

'Oooo-oooh! Someone's in a snippy mood,' retorted the computer.

'And,' carried on Gizmo pompously, ignoring Maxie, 'if he hadn't ignored the Intergalactic Travel and Transport Pact rules and regulations regarding . . .'

Maxie butted in heatedly. 'When you two have quite finished trashing Harvey do you think you could spare the time to help me figure out how to lock the doors so the command bridge won't be overrun by a bunch of deadly poison-gas-farting garbage aliens, forcing Gizmo and me to die a disgustingly gross and gruesome death?!'

There was a nano-beat as Gizmo took this in. Then he cried 'Good idea!' and frantically starting searching the engineering desk for the door controls.

Maxie rolled her eyes, sighed heavily, pushed up her sleeves and went over to help him.

'Do you actually know what you're doing?'

'Um . . . no,' confessed Gizmo, frowning. But that wasn't going to stop him.

Maxie pointed to a row of green and red switches along the top.

'What do those do?'

'No idea,' said Gizmo, busily switching them all ON and OFF and accidentally turning on the windscreen wipers on all three vision screens.

SCHWIP, SCHWOP, SCHWIP, SCHWOP!

'Oh, good grief,' groaned Maxie. 'What do these do?' she continued, indicating a series of large orange buttons.

'Haven't a clue,' said Gizmo, pounding away at them feverishly and turning the *Toxic Spew*'s headlights on to FULL BEAM and its fog lights on to METEOR SMOG MODE.

'And that?' asked Maxie, indicating a large yellow dial.

'Who knows?' said Gizmo, instantly grabbing it and yanking it round to HIGH. Rock music instantly blared out around the bridge followed by a jaunty jingle: 'Radio Galaxy Forty-three-Beeee-eeee!'

'Well obviously, not you!' snapped Maxie cranking the dial to OFF. 'Computer? Do you know how to lock the doors to the command bridge?' she yelled.

'Yes, thank you,' it replied smugly.

'WELL, LOCK THE DOORS!' bellowed Maxie and Gizmo furiously.

'Did I hear a please?' asked the computer.

'I'm warning you . . .' snarled Maxie menacingly.

Lights flickered on and off the computer's console then there was a soft

CLUNK!

and a red sign above the doors lit up. It read

'Thank you,' said Maxie.

'My pleasure,' replied the computer sarcastically and bleeped off.

CHAPTER TWENTY-ONE

Sick buckets in sickbay

By the time the others had hauled Scrummage to the sickbay, Harvey was beginning to feel horribly sick, and Snuffles was sneezing damply.

Yargillians have no sense of smell and so Yargal wasn't affected by the Junk Skunks' stench, and neither was Nerdie of course, but Scrummage was still out cold. Between the three of them they managed to heave him onto the bed and Yargal plugged up the Medi-Monitor. Harvey waited anxiously to see what it would say. There were a few blips and blibbles and a couple of lights blinked on and off softly. Then a message appeared on the screen. It read:

HE'LL BE FINE

BUT YOU'RE GOING TO NEED

A LOT OF SICK BUCKETS

'I don't want a sickbay covered in vomit!' announced Yargal, poking around the cupboards in a frenzy, and digging out a couple of grubby grey metal buckets.

Harvey looked round the filthy state of the room. The walls, floor and even the ceiling were covered in all sorts of grimy globs of muck and slimy smears of stuff, which to Harvey looked suspiciously like sick. There was so much of it Harvey wondered if that was why it was called the 'sickbay'.

Fortunately Harvey has a strong stomach. But he was still feeling pretty rough. So Yargal offered him some medicine. She took what looked like a large metal pen out of a drawer. Harvey knew it was a JabPen full of medicine. He'd seen her stab Scrummage with one before – and the huge Rubbish Officer had instantly slithered to the floor like a jelly.

'What's in it?' he asked.

'No idea,' said Yargal. 'But it always seems to work.'

'Er, no thanks,' said Harvey.

'Or there's this?' suggested Yargal, holding up a plastic bottle of alarming looking thick green gooey liquid, and a large grubby spoon.

Rather impressively, the medicine managed to look like bogies, ear gunk, and with a hint of dandruff, all at the same time.

'It's Astrofen combined with Spacepol to make a powerful Spacebiotic. It's AntiGag, AntiVomit and AntiPuke. Perfect really,' she announced unscrewing the top.

'Again, what's in it?' cried Harvey, backing away as a smell of stinky socks and canned dog food escaped the bottle.

Yargal looked at the label. She frowned as

she struggled to read the words, which were long and, frankly, ridiculously complicated. Then, taking a deep breath, she had a go at reading them out to Harvey, as confidently as she could, trying to make it sound like she knew what they all meant.

'Well, there's some Anti-hist-rich-dox-hi-drate and some Anti-flis-tec-ek-x-etit and also some Anti-bis-tic-box-et and . . .' she struggled on bravely, avoiding the suspicious look in Harvey's eye, and took a run at the last one, 'and some Ant-histi-click-check-dio-sid,' she finished triumphantly.

'Again,' said Harvey, pulling a face, 'no thanks.'

'It's banana flavour,' tempted Yargal.

'I'm feeling better already,' lied Harvey.

'Don't worry. I have a plan,' lied Harvey.

'So, what are you going to do?' asked Yargal, reluctantly putting the bottle back.

As a matter of fact, Harvey had absolutely no idea. But he didn't want to admit that to Yargal.

(Look – I don't want to give you the wrong impression of Harvey here. It's not that he wanted to pretend he's cleverer than he is. It's just that Yargal has a tendency to panic – you might have noticed. And she also has a tendency to splatter everyone with disgusting grey snot while she does so.)

'Don't worry. I have a plan,' lied Harvey, again.

(Look – again, I don't want to give you the wrong impression of Harvey here. It's not that he's a cunning and clever liar. But he can be a good liar – when he needs to be. Which, since he joined the Toxic Spew, is turning out to be disturbingly often.)

'I'll come with you,' volunteered Nerdie.

'Thanks,' replied Harvey gratefully. He hadn't

been exactly looking forward to taking on the Junk Skunks all by himself, but he wasn't going to put one of this teammates, er . . . crew members at risk, that was for sure. But of course the droid wouldn't be affected by the toxic fumes from the stinky critters at all. Although, given that the Nerdbot's functions were: tidying, cleaning and making galaxy-class intergalactic coffee, Harvey wasn't sure how much help he would be.

'Take Snuffles with you,' suggested Yargal.

'But what about the smell?' asked Harvey, reaching out protectively towards the space dog and scratching him behind the ears. Snuffles nudged Harvey's hand with his great big meatball of a nose.

'He's a Hazard Hunting Hound! He's trained for this kind of thing,' replied Yargal. 'But if you're worried I can give you something to protect both of you from the smell. Well . . . a bit.' And she started rummaging in drawer.

'Er . . . its not medicine is it?' said Harvey anxiously.

'Don't be ridiculous!' snorted Yargal, finding what she was looking for. 'Here, have one of these each.' And she handed Harvey what was possibly, no, make that definitely, two of the tattiest, filthiest, smelliest and most astonishingly stained bandages Harvey had ever seen.

Oh, gross, he thought. But it was probably better than nothing. So he wrapped the cloth around his nose and mouth while Yargal did the same for Snuffles.

'Good luck, Captain!' exclaimed Yargal, suddenly grabbing him and giving him a disgustingly soggy hug that left him damp round the edges. Then she wiped a few sticky grey tears from her googly eyes with her apron, and a long string of greasy snot from her nose with a tentacle.

A sudden, horrible thought hit Harvey like a punch in the stomach. 'Where's Gordon?' he cried, realising that the baby Gordonzola wouldn't be able to defend himself from the Junk Skunks.

'OH NO! I left him in the galley!' screamed

Yargal. 'All on his own! Captain!' she cried, waggling her eyes and tentacles hysterically, 'you've got to save him! He's only a baby!'

'Don't panic,' said Harvey. 'I'm on my way . . .' he yelled to Yargal over his shoulder as he ran off, followed by Snuffles and Nerdie.

(I'm not sure if you're the sort of person who likes lists, but if you are, then here's Harvey's To Do List:

- *Rescue Gordon*
- *Find Junk Skunks*
- *Catch Junk Skunks*
- *Save Toxic Spew and Everyone on Board*
- *Check Maxie and Gizmo*
- *Check Yargal and Scrummage*
- *Feed Snuffles*
- *Brush Teeth*
- *Go to Bed*

Blimey – bet that's busier than your day, huh!)

'That young man doesn't realise how brave he is!' sniffed Yargal. Then she turned her attention to Scrummage, who was beginning to come round and make the sort of noises that sounded very much like he was going to be violently, revoltingly, and monumentally sick.

You know, like

BLUPP, BLUPPP, BLUUUUUP . . .

and

BLEEEURRGH!

CHAPTER TWENTY-TWO

Harvey heads off heroically

Heroically, Harvey and the Hazard Hunting Hound headed off, with Nerdie close behind, to rescue Gordon, track down the rampaging Junk Skunks, *and* to save the *Toxic Spew*!

'So what's your plan, Captain?' asked the Nerdbot 1000, whizzing down the corridor alongside Harvey, on its metal wheel.

'I don't actually have one!' confessed Harvey, sprinting along, with Snuffles lolloping along at his heels. Fortunately Harvey can run and think at the same time. (Aha! That'll be why he's such a talented footballer.)

But what should he do first? Rescue Gordon or catch the Junk Skunks? Then, brilliantly, he realised that capturing the garbage pests would actually be saving Gordon *at the same time*! And that, astonishingly, there was one member of the *Toxic Spew* crew who was both fully trained and brilliant at their job.

So he stopped suddenly and turned to the huge hound. 'Snuffles!' he ordered. 'Seek!'

Snuffles abruptly stopped too, sat on the deck and looked at Harvey, waggling his ears and eyebrows in utter confusion.

AROUU?!

Harvey realised he didn't know the right command word. Obviously it wasn't 'Seek'. 'Er . . . Track!' he tried, then, 'Hunt!' and 'Find!' but Snuffles just sat there doing the ears and eyebrows wiggling thing. It was very cute – but not much use. Then finally, and desperately, Harvey tried, 'Er . . . Fetch?' Snuffles shot to his feet, took one almighty and, scrabbling like a demented werewolf, promptly pelted off down a side passageway.

It wasn't difficult to follow the Junk Skunks' trail. There was the eye-wateringly awful stench, the dollops of green goo splattered on the walls and deck, the gag-makingly ghastly stink, the pockets of swirling yellow fog, and oh, did I mention the hideously horrendous pong?

Harvey and Nerdie raced after Snuffles. They tore around the toilets, past a cosy chill-out room full of beanbags (that Harvey didn't even know existed) through the crews' quarters, in and out of the lifts, down to the lower deck and back up again. They sped along countless filthy corridors, past the Vacuum Control Room, the Engine Room (twice – and from different directions), under and over both Rear Rocket Blasters and almost straight through the exit pod and into outer space!

On the way Harvey scooped up anything he saw lying about that might be useful in a scuffle with a bunch of badly behaved and vile-smelling Junk Skunks.

(Just so you know, he grabbed:

- *a pair of Scrummage's goggles,*
- *a dirty sock,*
- *an old woollen glove,*
- *and the lid from a battered metal dustbin.*

Of course, he'd have been a lot better off with:

- *a complete Anti Junk Skunks 9091-2.0 Kit with*
- *a full face Gas Mask 7000,*
- *full-length gum boots,*
- *a full protective suit,*

and

- *a full spray can of SKUNKFUNK 5000*

(which kills off the stench)

But hey, you can't have everything.)

As they rounded a corner, Harvey realised to his horror, the trail was leading towards the galley where the baby Gordonzola was *all alone*! He kicked himself.

(No, not literally. Ever tried running and kicking yourself at the same time? Ridiculously tricky, isn't it?)

Yargal and Scrummage would never forgive him if the baby Gordonzola was hurt, and worse, he would never forgive himself.

'Gordon!' cried Harvey as they charged into the galley, but the baby alien was nowhere to be seen.

(Phew! Thank goodness for that!)

Junk Skunks on the other hand, could be seen

SPLOOG

everywhere – raiding the kitchen cupboards and squatting on the counters, ripping open packets, cramming food into their mouths and generally gobbling everything up quickly speedily, greedily, and very, very happily.

And they weren't going to give up without a fight . . .

CHAPTER TWENTY-THREE

Battle in the galley

SPLAT!

Harvey gasped as a lump of cold damp mozzarella walloped into his face, and dribbled down his chin.

SLURP! GULP!

went Snuffles, helpfully, instantly wolfing down the cheese and cleaning Harvey's face at the same time. (Oh, yuk. How absolutely gross.)

'Snuffles! OFF!' ordered Harvey, pushing the hound away.

'Look out!' creaked Nerdie.

Harvey ducked. A yoghurt pot, two strawberry cheesecakes and a chocolate mousse sailed over his head and exploded on the wall.

'Take cover!' yelled Harvey, as the Junk Skunks lobbed several large cans of pilchards at them.

CLANG! CLANK!

The tins crashed against Nerdie's metal body but bounced off harmlessly.

Pulling on the goggles, and shielding himself with the dustbin lid, Harvey commando-rolled across the galley deck and yanked open a cupboard. Grabbing a metal bucket and jamming it onto his head, he valiantly grasped the best weapon he could find – a non-stick frying pan.

(Maybe not the obvious choice – but it was that or a pair of tatty plastic toast tongs, OK?)

CLANG!

A tin of pineapple chunks clunked against Harvey's metal bucket, er, helmet. Followed by a family-size pack of double chocolate chip and rhubarb custard cookies.

SCRUNCH!

And then the skunks launched a ferocious, all-out assault with dozens of juicy quarter-pounder hamburgers . . .

DROOL, SLOBBER!

went Snuffles, diving in with his mouth open, and

THWACK, WHACK!

went Harvey, batting the burgers away furiously with his frying pan.

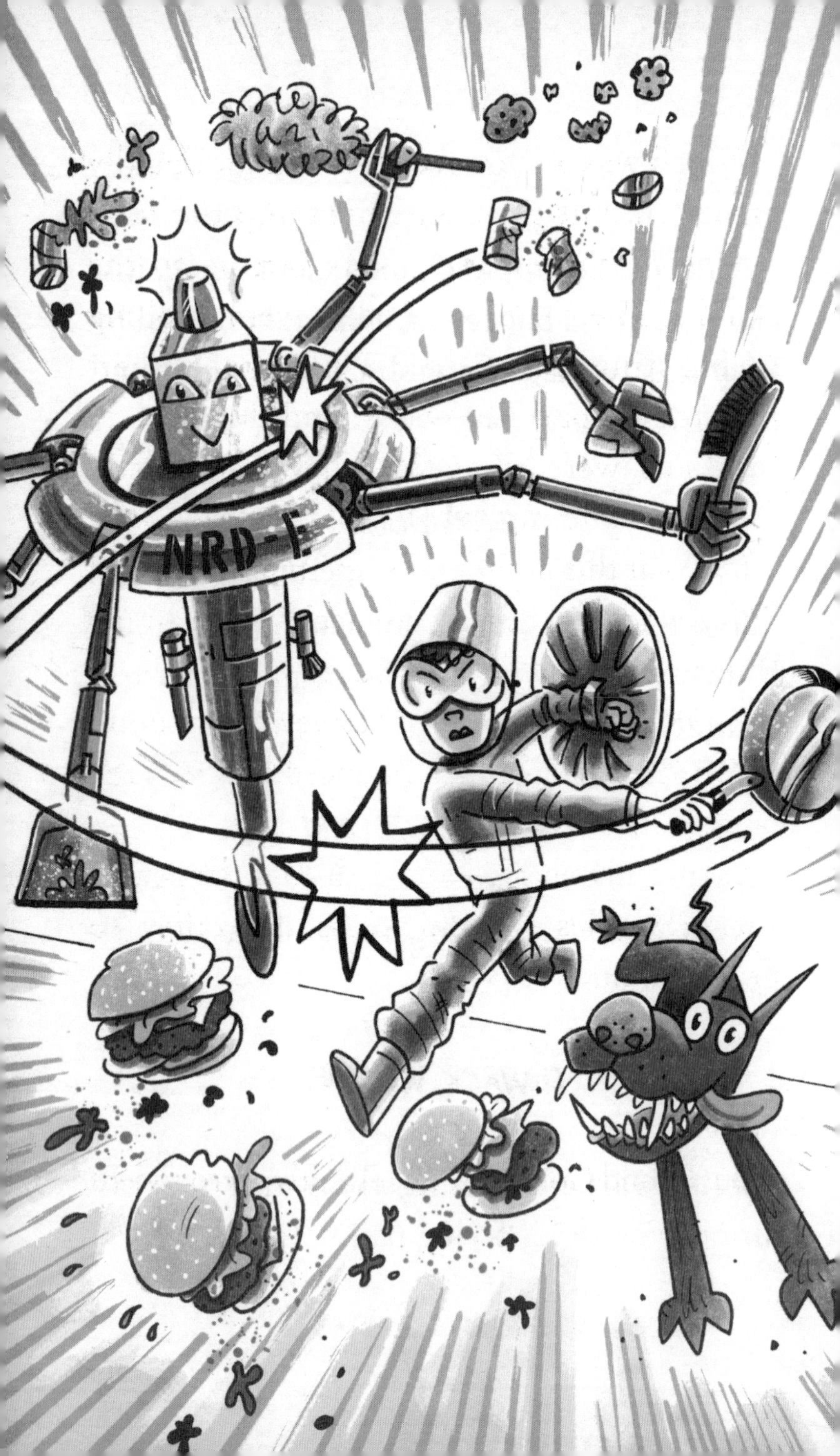
NRD-E

Which was all very brave and undoubtedly great fun, but the excitement and the food – *especially* the food – was getting to the skunks. Their rubbery bodies were swelling to bursting point, like a bunch of over-pumped-up party balloons, and their, er . . . rear ends, were filling the galley with ghastly green goo and noxious yellow gas!

It was at this point that something small and fluffy waddled across the deck, wagging its little nappy-clad bottom merrily.

'GORDON!' exclaimed Harvey. 'Noooooo!'

Too late! The skunks pounced towards the baby Gordonzola!

Baring his shark-like teeth in a ferocious snarl, Snuffles sprang across the galley to protect him,

GRRRRR, WOOOF!

But he and Gordon were instantly surrounded!

Harvey's rubbish idea

An outstanding rubbish idea suddenly struck Harvey.

Bravely brandishing his non-stick frying pan, he yelled to Nerdie, 'Drive the skunks into the corner – to the garbage chute!'

'Stand back, Captain,' rasped the Nerdbot 1000, rapidly unclipping cleaning attachments with all of its six metal claws at once. Then it *charged* at the Junk Skunks ferociously wielding, with awesome accuracy, its:

- telescopic cobweb brush,
- litter grabber,
- long-handled broom,
- matching dustpan and brush, and
- fluffy pink feather duster.

And within moments the droid had rounded the stinky little aliens up and herded them backwards and onto the trap door to the rubbish shaft. Calmly, Harvey pulled the lever to OPEN and the pongy little pests tumbled harmlessly down into the cargo hold, landing on the pile of garbage the *Toxic Spew* had emptied from *Waitless*. Then he pulled the lever to SHUT, trapping the troublesome cosmic critters in the garbage hold.

'Yahoo!' cried Harvey, doing a high-five with Nerdie.

CLANG!

'OWW!' yelped Harvey, doubling over in agony.

(Seriously?!

Look, I don't mean to be rude and I know you don't have a lot of domestic robots on your little planet, do you, but I would've thought that even someone from Earth would be smart enough to work out that high-fiving metal body parts really, really hurts!)

Harvey clamped his throbbing hand under his armpit, eyes watering and screaming silently under his breath.

'I'm sorry, sir,' croaked Nerdie rustily. 'Are you all right?'

Harvey took a deep breath and held it. 'I'm fine,' he finally managed to squeak. 'Apart from the fact I think I've broken my hand!'

'I know! How about a refreshing squirt of SmelloGel?' suggested Nerdie, spraying Harvey all over with a fine mist of beeswax and vanilla-scented multi-surface polish.

'How's that supposed to help?' cried Harvey coughing and spluttering.

'It says it "Shines and restores as good as new"!' said the cleaning robot, reading the label on the tin.

'That's for things, not humans!'

'Is there a big difference?' asked Nerdie.

'Yes!' cried Harvey.

'Ah,' rasped Nerdie, and his six metal extending arms drooped sadly.

CHAPTER TWENTY-FOUR

Harvey to the bridge

Harvey ordered Snuffles to stay and look after Gordon. Then he suggested Nerdie clean up the disgusting mess the Junk Skunks had made all over the *Toxic Spew* – starting with the galley. The Nerdbot 1000 cheered up immediately.

'It'll be my pleasure, sir!' he said, efficiently reeling out his VoltaVacuum attachment and taking out an industrial-sized, pump-action, plastic tub of Mountain Breeze and Wild Cherry air freshener.

Harvey belted back up to the bridge to tell Maxie and Gizmo it was all clear. Knowing that the toxic stench of the skunks would hang around the ship for some time yet, he left Yargal's grubby bandage over his nose and mouth until he got to the safety of the bridge.

As he pelted along the last straight of corridor, his space boots squelching and sticking to the filthy deck as he ran, he allowed himself to feel a bit pleased with himself for having dealt with the Junk Skunks.

Like a lot of people who are *outstandingly* good at something (football, in his case), Harvey was usually pretty modest about it. But then, let's face it, when the rest of your team are clapping you on the back and voting you 'Man of the Match', and you've just scored your third hat-trick of the season, you don't need to brag about it, do you?

But on this occasion, to be honest, Harvey was looking forward to seeing the look on Maxie's face when he burst onto the bridge to say it was safe.

It was a shame he wasn't also looking forward at where he was going.

SLAM!

DOOOOF!

Harvey ran slap bang into the bridge doors and poleaxed painfully onto the deck. He'd expected them to open automatically, like they always did, promptly and with a satisfying

SCHWOOOSH . . .

They hadn't.

Harvey staggered to his feet and pounded on the doors. 'Maxie? Gizmo?' he shouted. 'Open up!' There was no reply.

Harvey to the rescue

He ran to the nearest ship intercom (which turned out to be the one just outside the toilets).

'Harvey to the command bridge. Are you there?' he cried.

(I hate to interrupt at this exciting moment, but is it me, or does that seem a completely absurd question?

I mean:

a) Where did he think the command bridge would be? Wandering around the ship on its own? Gone out for a pizza? In a parallel universe having crossed the time space portal wotsit thingy to another world?

And

b) Even if it was where he had left it (which it was) how did he think the command bridge could actually answer him? Huh? It's just a room full of technical kit and other cosmic clutter and a handful of tatty old seats, for crying out loud.)

Since there was no reply, Harvey tried the computer.

'Captain Harvey!' it replied in its digital voice. 'Is that really you? What a lovely surprise! I thought you'd died. Like the bridge crew,' it finished casually.

'What?!' exclaimed Harvey.

'At least, I think they're dead. They look pretty dead to me,' it announced cheerfully. 'They've gone all limp and they haven't moved for ages.'

'Open the bridge doors!' barked Harvey.

'Are you sure?'

'Yes!'

'Don't you think you're a teeny, tiny bit young to go onto the command bridge all on your own and discover your crew mates slumped dead and lifeless in their seats?

'No, now OPEN THE DOORS!' yelled Harvey.

'Is that OPEN THE DOORS, please?' snipped the computer.

'NO! It's OPEN-THE-DOORS-AND-THAT'S-AN-ORDER!' bawled Harvey.

'Tut, tut! Manners!' sniffed the computer.

Harvey tore along the filthy corridor and onto the bridge.

SCHWOOOOSH . . .

Maxie and Gizmo were both collapsed at their desks. The skunk stink had seeped onto the bridge through the air vents.

'Maxie!' cried Harvey, rushing over to the pilot. To his enormous relief she was alive and breathing, and to be accurate, dribbling a bit. He tried shaking her, but he couldn't wake her. She was out cold. And so was Gizmo.

And worse . . .

The *Toxic Spew* was hurtling through space, completely out of control!

And even worse . . .

Glancing out of the front vision screen, Harvey's blood froze . . . and his heart leapt into the back of his throat.

A *colossal* spaceberg was looming towards them. It was so close Harvey could clearly see a snow-covered mountain spewing out enormous lava balls. You know, those mega-terrifying, blubblering-blue, ice-cold, freeze-exterminating intergalactic type ones.

And much, much worse . . . they were ALL GOING TO DIE!

CHAPTER TWENTY-FIVE

Spaceberg!

Harvey hauled Maxie out of her seat and into the captain's chair. Then he radioed Yargal and ordered her to come to the bridge – *immediately*.

(Good luck with that, Captain!
With a top speed of a JelloNovian Racing Snail, you might not want to hold your breath until she gets there.)

Harvey was desperately worried about his crew, but he had to focus on saving the ship.

He took over the pilot's seat, forced himself to stay calm, and scanned the flight controls.

(Why? He's no idea what any of them do!)

'Computer, help!' he ordered.

'Well, this is fun!' announced the computer chirpily. 'Thundering towards a humungous spaceberg at a thrilling Cosmic Speed 8! Wheeeee! Unfortunately, there will be a tremendous explosion blowing the ship into a gazillion little pieces.

'But, on the upside, it will

a) be spectacular,
b) all be over very quickly, and
c) you won't feel a thing!'

Battling to keep his temper, Harvey asked the computer if it could actually do anything to help, like maybe fly the ship.

'I am a galaxy-class 75b SpaceCorp computer

with a CosmicCore processor and 215 megatronbyte boogle memory – not an AutoAstronaut!' it snapped, huffily.

'Then search the Outernet and find out how to do it!' ordered Harvey.

'Oh, good idea!' said the computer, brightly. 'It's when you come up with clever ideas like that I see why they made you captain. Now, what shall I type in the little search box?'

'I don't know!' yelled Harvey, finally losing it. 'Try: "How-to-stop-a-spaceship-thundering-towards-a-humungous-spaceberg-at-a-*thrilling*-Cosmic-Speed-8.com!"'

'Righty ho! Will do! Don't go away!' it joked.

SCHWOOOSH . . .

The bridge doors slid open and Yargal slurped in. She stared open-mouthed at the spaceberg, which was now terrifyingly close. Then, still with her mouth open she screamed, 'Aaaaaaaargh!'

'Yargal, calm down and help Maxie,' commanded Harvey briskly.

'Shouldn't I help Gizmo first – he is senior and I'm sure he'd say that according to the Intergalactic Travel and Transport Pact rules . . .'

'Can Gizmo fly the ship?' cut in Harvey.

'No.' said Yargal.

'Then start with Maxie!'

DO NOT PRESS!

While Yargal slurped her way slowly over to the Pilot Officer who was still slumped in Harvey's chair, the computer suddenly bleeped on happily.

'Captain,' it said excitedly, 'you'll be delighted to hear I've found an *excellent* step-by-step SpaceChat guide on how to pilot spaceships! So just listen carefully and follow the instructions.

Step 1: Add lots of GasoLime goo to the fuel tank.

Step 2: Turn the starter key to the ON position.
Step 3: Hold up trigger (A).
Step 4: Turn wheel (B) to where you want to go . . .'

'This isn't helping at all!' spluttered Harvey at the flight controls, as the monumentally colossal spaceberg loomed menacingly nearer and nearer.

'Wait . . . there's a bit about doing an Emergency Stop! Apparently you hit the big red button marked DO NOT PRESS.'

Urgently, Harvey scanned the flight desk for a button marked DO NOT PRESS. He found it, in between one labelled DON'T TOUCH and another one that read DON'T EVEN THINK ABOUT IT.

'Seriously?' said Harvey, his hand hovering over the Emergency Stop control button.

'Yup!'

'Are you sure?'

'Yup!'

'Completely and totally, 100 per cent, sure?'

'Yup!'

Closing his eyes and crossing his fingers, Harvey's hand smacked down hard on the big red button.

KA-POW THWACK!

An enormous airbag, like a giant blow-up duvet, erupted out of the flight desk, knocking him clean off his feet and smothering him.

'Captain,' cried Yargal. 'Are you all right?'

'Weff, I'm fwine!' came Harvey's muffled voice from under the mound of material.

Desperately he battled with the mountain of bloated cloth, but it was impossible to grab and he couldn't see what he was doing. It would have been a lot easier to wrestle his way out of a bouncy castle, blindfolded and in the dark.

And all the while the ship jumped and juddered violently, and a horrible screeching noise came from the booster engines, and

AIR-B
DO NOT PRESS!

another even more horrible screeching noise came from Yargal.

'Aaaaaargh!!!!'

Oooops!

Harvey just managed to clamber out from under the enormous airbag in time to see the *Toxic Spew* finally, wonderfully, marvellously and totally – come to a shuddering, jolting stop!

'Oh, well done!' said the computer, and Harvey let out a huge sigh of relief.

'I really didn't think you were going to manage to stop the ship!' chattered the computer cheerfully. 'Of course the enormous spaceberg is still rocketing towards us fatally fast, and spewing out mega-terrifying, blubblering-blue, ice-cold, freeze-exterminating lava balls and we're going to smash into it anyhow,' it continued heartlessly. 'But it was a nice try. Now, how about a quick game before you die?

'Captain,' wailed Yargal. 'I don't want a quick game before I die. I don't want to die at all!'

But Harvey wasn't listening. It wasn't that he wasn't interested in Yargal's tragically pathetic last wish. It was more that Harvey didn't want to die either and was too busy

a) trying not to, by
b) having a brilliant idea.

'*A game – that's it!*' thought Harvey. At home he'd completed both Fly Galactic Ships NOW (Volume 1) and Fly More Galactic Ships NOW (Volume 2). A real spaceship couldn't be *that* different, surely. Desperately he dragged the airbag off the flight controls.

Er . . . yes it could.

The games flight controls weren't anything like those in the real flight desk front of him. *Hang on, what about Helicopter Havoc?* wondered Harvey, desperately. *That's based on a real flight desk*. He sat back down in the pilot's seat.

If he could just work out how to turn left . . . or right . . . or go up . . . or down . . . or *anything* other than hanging around doing nothing and waiting for 'Sudden Death By Spaceberg'!

Frantically, he started switching switches, pounding buttons and hauling levers. And, to his enormous relief, and even greater surprise the *Toxic Spew* began to move. Unfortunately, it went forwards – bringing the head-on collision with the spaceberg even closer! Oooops.

CHAPTER TWENTY-SIX

More speed!

Meanwhile Yargal was merrily slapping Maxie with her soggy tentacles.

THWACK SPLAT!

THWACK SPLAT!

It wasn't a medically approved method – but it seemed to work. Maxie's eyes flickered open.

THWACK SPLAT!

went Yargal once more, just for luck.

'Ow!' yelped Maxie. 'Pack it in!' Then, looking around the bridge, still dazed, she suddenly realised Harvey was at the flight desk. 'What are you doing?' she screamed, struggling to sit up.

'Flying the ship!' replied Harvey coolly.

'But you don't know how to!' she exclaimed, scrambling to her feet.

'No, but I'm working on it.'

Maxie tried to stand, but her legs buckled under her.

(She actually said a very rude word, which I am shocked to find she even knows, and no, I'm not going to say what it was.)

Feverishly flicking switches and fiddling with dials, Harvey put the ship's manifold magnetos to FULL, slid the sideways booster thrusters to ON, turned up the turbo anti-torque throttles and let out the cyclic clutch and pitch control lever.

(Or something equally impressive. And no, I don't know how to fly the ship either).

Then he confidently grasped the flight control stick and boldly yanked it to the left. To everyone's relief (and total amazement) the *Toxic Spew* began to veer slowly left, and edge away from the spaceberg!

'Congratulations, Captain!' cried the computer. 'We're going to miss the spaceberg after all! Well done!

'Wait! Oh no, we're not. We're just going to clip the edge and completely explode on impact! Oh, bad luck, sir! Hey ho, cheerio everyone!' it finished, gobsmackingly tactlessly.

'More speed!' yelled Maxie to Harvey.

Harvey cranked the controls from FAST to VERY FAST, still hauling the joystick, and the ship itself, hard left.

They held their breath, eyes fixed on the vast front vision as the *Toxic Spew* juuuuust slipped past the massive spaceberg with a nano-smidge to spare! Maxie watched mega impressed, and supa-mega relieved, as Harvey steered the ship safely off into outer space.

'Captain, that was AWESOME!' she announced, and Harvey grinned at her.

Gobsmacking greed

Yargal had started happily doing the THWACK, SPLAT! routine on Gizmo. At which point Scrummage arrived on the bridge. He was feeling much better and immediately offered to help by giving Gizmo a really hard slap, or two.

'No,' said Harvey firmly, as Maxie snorted with laughter and rolled her eyes.

And then, as soon as Gizmo had recovered, Yargal slid off to make everyone a celebratory pizza.

So, a short while later, they all sat on the command bridge of the *Toxic Spew* munching pizzas while Nerdie made them all coffee.

Much to everyone's surprise, Maxie was actually letting Harvey pilot the ship. She'd carefully plotted the route for him to follow, avoiding the black hole, three speed cameras, two sets of traffic lights, the one-way system, and a dead end.

They were contentedly heading back to *Waitless*. Partly because they were meeting InterPlanetary Pest Control there but mostly because the manager of the intergalactic super store had said they could have anything they liked from the shop as payment for removing the Junk Skunks and emptying the garbage. I repeat: *anything they liked*. What an idiot.

(Please don't read this list. It's gobsmackingly greedy.

Maxie upgraded the flight desk with a brand new multi-coloured cybersonic jump drive control.

Gizmo wanted a talking repair kit that tells you which tool to choose and how to use it, and a Cosmic Spanner 7017

(an unbreakable all-in-one spanner, screwdriver, pen and spoon).

Scrummage chose food – starting with biggest bag of Hot Chilli Space Chips, not just in the shop – but in the Entire Known Universe, and Beyond.

Harvey got Cosmic Catastrophe (the original game plus booster pack). Billed as 'educational fun for the whole crew', players have to tackle a series of difficult and dangerous intergalactic missions before their imaginary spaceship self-destructs. In all honesty he might as well try to teach his crew how to knit a black hole.

Snuffles drove everyone nuts with a really annoying squeaky chew bone.

Finally, Yargal picked a Supersonic Speedy 2000 Automatic Spatula and six oven gloves (which Scrummage thought were tentacle warmers!) and a litter tray for Gordon.)

Harvey had handed the flight controls back over to Maxie and was sitting back in the captain's chair, looking forward to some keepie-uppie with the zero gravity football after tea, when the computer bleeped importantly.

'I think I've found your home planet, Captain,' it announced confidently. 'Is this Earth?' it asked, displaying an image of something that looked a bit like a yellow crescent moon.

'No,' said Harvey. 'That's a banana.'

'Ah,' cringed the computer.

'Earth,' creaked Nerdie rustily, 'is a small, round green and blue planet.'

'Yes!' cried Harvey excitedly. 'It is! Do you know where it is?'

'Yes, it's in a mythical galaxy called The Milky Way,' replied the robot.

‘It’s not mythical!’ exclaimed Harvey.

‘It must be,’ snorted Maxie. ‘Honestly, “The Milky Way”! What sort of name is that for a galaxy? It sounds more like a chocolate bar!’

The entire crew burst out laughing – especially Harvey (but *excluding* Nerdie who isn’t programmed with a laugh function).

Looks like Captain Harvey Drew is stuck on the *Toxic Spew* for another rubbish adventure with the Bin Men from Outer Space. Flickering spew!

TOP SECRET!

FOR CAPTAIN'S EYES ONLY!

FLIGHT MANUAL FOR INTERGALACTIC GARBAGE SPACESHIP THE *TOXIC SPEW*

CONTENTS

TOP TEN MOST DEADLY GARBAGE PESTS IN THE ENTIRE KNOWN UNIVERSE, AND BEYOND

1. **Giant Green Killerleg GungeBeetles:** From the Cesspit and Cesspool Moons in the Gunkball Cluster. [by Booty]

2. **Mutant BeastyBix:** Savage, mutated, glow-in-the-dark, orange biscuits. (They launch the ultimate SnackAttack). [by Derpy dog Teenyweeny LMJ]

3. **SlughogSpays from Vampirus 7:** Prickly bouncy balls that suck your blood until you're just skin and bones.

[by Teenyweeny KW + Teenyweeny ID + Teenyweeny LS]

4. **Junk Skunks:** Deadly poison-gas-farting critters.

Warning!

5. **Fluffcroobes from Fluff-i Minox:** Extremely cute with bright yellow fluff and dark purple eyes. But so poisonous you need protective armour. [by Teenyweeny, Teenyweeny LMJ/LC]

6. **Kicklesaps:** These trash-munching fiends lie in wait and then explode in your face. Pointless really. [by Teenyweeny SP]

PANIC!!

7. **Pink Killer Maggots from Venomoid Flux:** They pump you with poison, melt your insides and slurp you like soup.

8. **RavenousRubbishRats:** Grey with green spots and a spiky tail as long as a

lasso. Originally from the planet Rattus Uratus. But they had to leave - they ate it! [by Fancyfootball]

9. **SpitPots:** Trash-spitting aliens that communicate by sending electric bolts to one another. It megahurts if you get in the way. [by Teenyweeny]

WHAT?!

10. **SnotBugSlugs:** Green and pink with yellow stripes, they're poisonous to eat. (Not that you would unless you were bonkers, since they're about as appealing as a bucket of slime.) [by Lemonspacecurd5]

11. **Multi-headed Multi-coloured GooglieSpiders:** From the Star System Optica Spectacula. They crawl into your skull, bite your brain, and give you a galaxy-sized headache. [by Lemonspacecurd6 + rockersMP + Rockers GWS]

What?!? That's 11, not 10?!

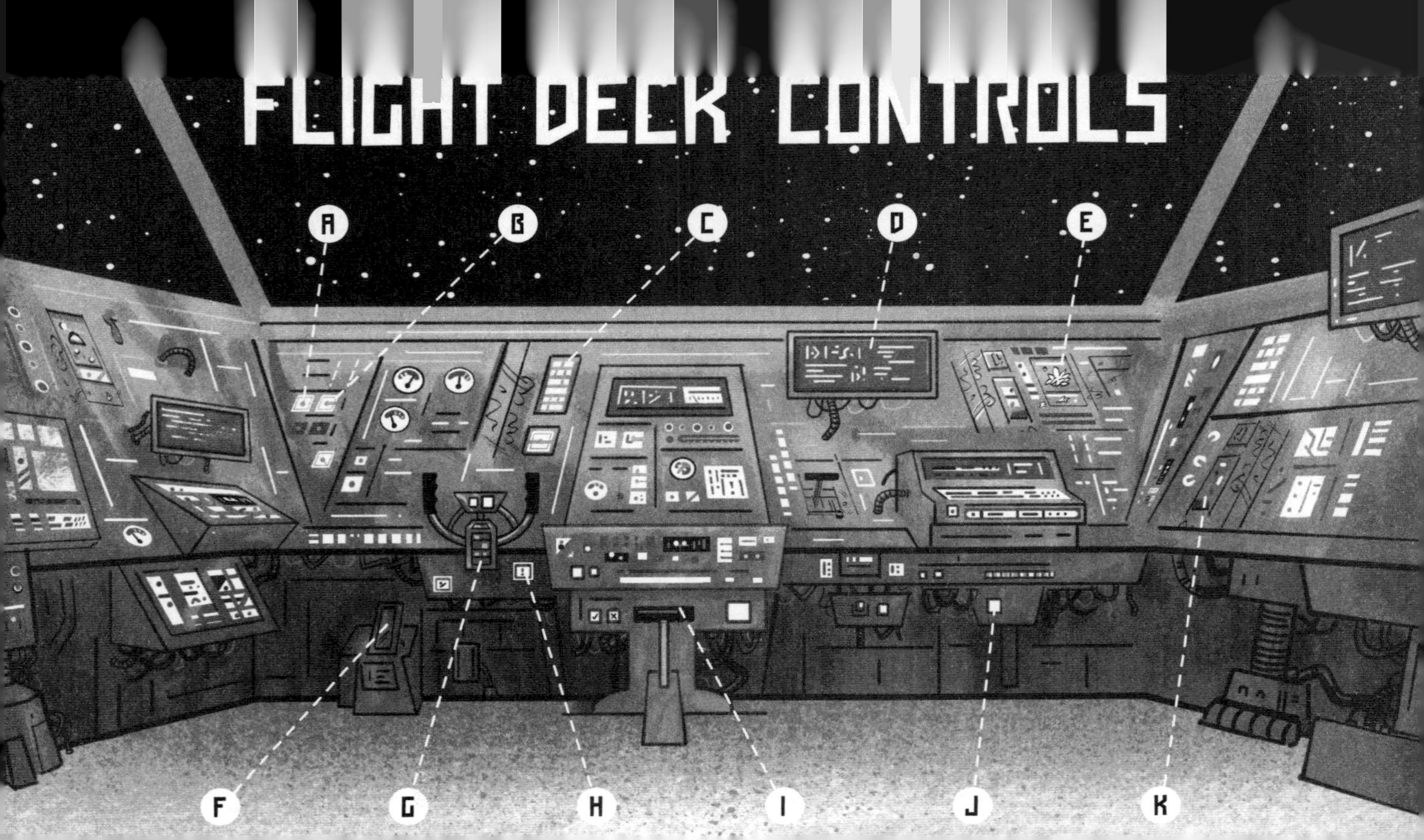

FLIGHT DECK CONTROLS
A
B
C
D
E
F
G
H
I
J
K

A	HYPERDRIVE GO BUTTON PRESS [by pool]
B	HYPERDRIVE STOP BUTTON [by pool]
C	INDESTRUCTIBLE SHIELD BUTTON [by pool]
D	A TOP OF THE LINE RAPDON: A SPEED MONITOR THAT IS ALSO A RADIO [by Cookieclicker2]
E	SELF-DESTRUCT BUTTON [by Lemonspacecurd 3]
F	PILOT EJECTOR BUTTON [by Isapop]
G	SUPERSONIC SPACE STEERING WHEEL,WITH BOOSTER CONTROLS [by Lemonspacecurd2 and Lemonspacecurd3]
H	OFF BUTTON [by AlienAttacker]
I	BRAKE LEVER [by Lemonspacecurd6 and Cookieclicker4]
J	INVISIBLE BUTTON [by pool]
K	EVERYBODY PANIC BUTTON [by Derpy dog Teenyweeny LMJ]

AUTHOR NOTE: Below is another example of a flight deck, drawn by exceptional artist Rockers GW-S.

Cas Says: "I really love all the ideas on this one! Especially the Self Destruct Button (oops!) and the compass – but it would have to be a 3D compass, with Up an Down as well. I love the fact it has a pressure gauge and a water gauge and a cruise control and a park control. And I want pizza, chocolate, OJ and sweets buttons fitted to my car dashboard controls IMMEDIATELY!!! AWESOME."

SAFETY EQUIPMENT

EXTREMELY IMPORTANT SAFETY EQUIPMENT

- All-Purpose Toxic Spew Proof Suits [by Lemonspacecurd2]
- Intergalactic Gas Mask 7000 [by Lemonspacecurd1]

OTHER LESS-IMPORTANT-BUT-STILL-USEFUL EQUIPMENT

- Maxie's old woollen gloves [by Fancyfootball]
- Scrummage's old pair of goggles [by Fancyfootball]
- A tin bucket (useful as a helmet) [by Rockets ED]

- A bin (makes a good shield) [by Cookieclicker4]
- Broken broom handle (good for whacking alien enemies) [by Cookieclicker4, Fancyfootball, Derpy dog Teenyweeny LMJ]
- Non-stick frying pan
- Ship's vacuum (missing plug) [by TheNuculearCreeper, dog lover, Cookieclicker2, Lemonspacecurd1]
- Tatty old plastic toast tongs [by Derpy dog Teenyweeny LMJ]

MEDICINES FOR YARGAL'S CABINET

- AntiGag, AntiVomit and AntiPuke medicine (to stop you feeling sick) [by gummypie15] BLEURGH
- Antihistrichdoxihidrate [by santa63]
- Antiflistecekxetit [by santa63]
- Antibisticboxet [by santa63]
- Antihisticlickcheckdiosid [by santa63]
- AntiSmellsBandages (to go over your nose so you can't smell) [by Rockers CH]
- Astrofen (pain relief) [by Fancyfootball]
- Banana medicine [by elmo10051] Yuk!
- Spacepol (to soothe pain) [by Rockers CH, FancyFootball]
- Space-o-biotics (to stop any symptoms coming back again) [by Rockers CH] DOUBLE YUK!
- Anti Poisonous Killer Maggot spray
- Stun Jab in 3 strengths: MildStun, SupaStun and SupaStunXtra

Vital!

Fat chance

ESSENTIAL KIT – INCLUDING REPAIR KIT

- An intergalactic titanium pickaxe [by fireball888]

No.

- A jet pack [by lozz]

No.

- A Wiffometer, to detect whether the smell of the garbage is:
  - a) hazardously horrendous or,
  - b) dangerously disgusting, or
  - c) fatally foul

Nope.

- A reinforced rubber toilet plunger;
- And one of those little scratch remover pens that are so handy for repairing all the little scrapes and nicks on the outside of the ship.

?!?

HOW TO SERVICE THE TOXIC SPEW

REFUELLING

1. Open intergalactic fuel cap.
2. Fill up the Toxic Spew with the Megatron 500 Insta-Refueller Pump.
3. Only use Three Star Premium GasoLime. [by TheNuculearCreeper, choklatechip, AlienAttacker]

Warning!

TOP UPS

1. Use the galactic air hose to pump up the bumper [by TheNuculearCreeper]
2. Refill glass cleaner tank with Scrub-O-Matic [by choklatechip, Fancyfootball]
3. Check levels of Sloppy Slime Oil and Super Charged Space Goo [by choklatechip]

Bagsy not...

TESTS

1. Check the intergalactic landing gear [by elmo10051]
2. Check the super hydronic brakes [by elmo10051]

   We wish...
3. Switch on and off directional lights
4. Check the windscreen wipers are still attached
5. Check mirrors are still attached (there should be two) and if so, polish with SmelloGel – beeswax and vanilla-scented multi-surface polish.

?!?

RULES AND REGULATIONS

The Crew of the Toxic Spew must abide by the following Intergalactic Travel and Transport Pact rules and regulations. And yes, that does mean you, Scrummage.

PANIC!!

If aliens get on the ship:

DON'T PANIC! Call the Intergalactic Traffic Police, try to keep away from the alien, throw pizzas in their face, take photos of the alien to identify it [by Derpy dog Teenyweeny LMJ]

If deadly dangerous aliens get on to the ship:

DON'T make eye contact. Keep calm. Make a trail of cheesy moon balls into the panic room and

DOUBLE PANIC!!

lock the alien in there until you reach land and leave them on a planet where they can do no harm [by Fancyfootball]

If the vacuum pump explodes:

DON'T lick your lips. Make sure that none of the crew are injured or stuck under any dust or rubbish. If there is any very smelly rubbish that living creatures can't live in until it has had chance to go away get to a safe place until it is all right to go back [by Fancyfootball]

WHAT?!

Replacing your captain:

DO find another captain. They can be quite useful.

Dumping dangerous rubbish:

DON'T – and if you do, then DON'T get caught.

Keeping critical controls clean:

Hey!

DO. Like captains, they can be quite useful.
NB: You DON'T have to keep your captain clean.

Huh?

Brawling on the bridge:

DON'T – it's rude and distracts the pilot.

Doing repairs outside a spaceship:

DO the repairs but DON'T unclip your lifeline!

Rescuing cargo ships:

DO rescue the ship and then bagsy the cargo – in that order.

Good idea...

Space pirates:

~~DON'T~~ PANIC! Space pirates are ruthless. You are all going to die. **PANIC!**

GUIDE TO ALIEN LANGUAGES

You can, of course, use Intergalactic GarbleTranslate, but if you find yourself without it then here are some key phrases you should learn:

Za Za Swiiflyumpcious = 'That's the best stench ever!'
A compliment paid when food served is deliciously pungent – like the whiff of a putrid fungal pie from the planet Pongoo! [by Booty]

!?

Gripeoooh = 'Oh my belly hurts - or maybe bellies!'

Usually uttered after scoffing a plate of putrid fungal pie. [by Booty]

Hey!

Doh poonicky! = 'Don't panic!'
[by Rockers CH and CB]

AMAZING!!

Suma bronga pazz = 'We bring pizza'
It also means 'We come with pizza' which is a phrase understood throughout the Entire Known Universe, and Beyond to mean: 'We come in peace'. [by Rockers CH and CB]

Sarada da = 'There was a problem with the alarm – we did pay!' [by Rockers MO]

Xcape NavisCosmos! = 'Abandon Spaceship!'

Aaaaaargh! = 'Aaaaaargh!'
In any language in the Entire Known Universe, and Beyond.

Space is so awsesome!!

TOP TEN MOST USEFUL SPACE FACTS [BY ROCKERS CH]

10) There are over 500,000 pieces of space junk in Earth's atmosphere

9) The sunset on Mars appears blue

8) If you could fly a plane to Pluto, the trip would take more than 800 years

7) All of space is completely silent

WOW!

6) Astronauts can't burp in outer space

5) Scientists believe that it rains diamonds on Neptune and Uranus

4) Space smells like raspberries

3) If you could put Saturn in water it would float

Cool!

2) The moon actually used to be a chunk of the Earth

?!?

1) A white hole is the opposite of a black hole. The white hole swallows up the black hole.

AWESOME LIMERICKS!

<u>'Gizmo' by kitten Teenyweeny TS</u>

There was a man called Gizmo
Who stubbed his very small toe
He yelled and he squealed
That's how he healed
And then he started to glow

<u>'Harvey' by Teenyweeny LJ and CJ</u>

There once was a boy, Harvey Drew
Who got teleported to the Toxic Spew.
It was full of old junk
That smelt like a skunk
But it did have a magnificent crew!

'Harvey' by Teenyweeny RM and LJ2

There was a captain named Harvey Drew
Who was terribly fond of his crew.
But his friend called Scrummage
Was always tempted to rummage
In the rubbish of the Toxic Spew

'Maxie' by Teenyweeny BC and ID

There once was an alien called Maxie
Who tried to catch a space taxi.
But then one day,
She flew away
And landed on the planet of Plaxi.

'Gordon' by Isapop

There once was an alien pet
He ate everything he could get
Gordon was his name
He seemed really tame
Until he attacked his vet

'Yargal and Snuffles' by Cas

Two aliens, Yargal and Snuffles,
Loved pizza with fishpaste and truffles.
Both ate and ate,
And emptied the plate,
Then decided they'd eaten enuffles!

'Sassy Space' by Teenyweeny BP and KW

Two planets called Venus and Mars
Both loved to eat chocolate bars
The sun was so jealous,
She burned those two fellas
So now they are both red dwarf stars.

A SPECIAL THANK YOU TO THE FOLLOWING STORY ADVENTURERS FOR SUPPORTING THIS BOOK:

Alex Digger
Becki Crossley
Buzz Lightyear
Connor Edwards
Emily-Jayne Bond
FancyFootball - Nancy
Godstowe School
Jake Downes
Jasen Booton
Jodi Leek
Leif Mae Johnson
Megan P

Ollie Layton
Rommi Temple
St Clement's CE Primary School Year 5
Tina Brown
Violet Ward

<u>SUPER STAR LIST Story Adventurers</u>:

Super Stars
ANobodyZ
Fancyfootball
Teenyweeny
Isapop
Booty
Twinkle
Weinbag

<u>STAR LIST Story Adventurers</u>:

Apple Pie Teenyweeny MP
Derpy dog Teenyweeny LMJ
kitten Teenyweeny TS
Lemonspacecurd7
POTATO Teenyweeny RM
Rockers

CONTRIBUTORS

Thanks to all of you that contributed your brilliant ideas to the making of this book!

Chapter One

Booty, Fancyfootball, Teenyweeny AJB, Teenyweeny JFL, Teenyweeny EL, Teenyweeny SP, Teenyweeny TS, Teenyweeny VW

Chapter Two

Alien Attacker, ANobodyZ, bean206, Fancyfootball, kitten Teenyweeny TS, loleypop, lolly pop Teenyweeny EI, lozz, Rockers, Rockers MO, tiara teenyweeny ajb

Chapter Three

AlienAttacker, Buzz Lightyear JRJR, choklatechip, CookieClicker1, CookieClicker2, CookieClicker4, CookieClicker5, CookieClicker6, cookie monster, Derpy dog Teenyweeny LMJ, Fancyfootball, Happy, Teenyweeny L.S, Lemonspacecurd4, lolly pop Teenyweeny EI, POTATO Teenyweeny RM, Rocker IM, Rockers MO, Rockers MP, TheNuculearCreeper

Chapter Four

elmo10051, games, Lemonspacecurd2, TheNuculearCreeper

(Manual): AlienAttacker, Cookieclicker2, Cookieclicker4, fireball888, Isapop, lozz, Lemonspacecurd2, Lemonspacecurd3, Lemonspacecurd6, Rockers CH, Rockers GW-S

Chapter Five

AlienAttacker, bean 206, choklatechip, Cookieclicker1, Cookieclicker5, cookie monster, elmo10051, Fancyfootball, fireball888, Lemonspacecurd2, Lemonspacecurd4, Lemonspacecurd6, lozz, puffle puff Teenyweeny BC, Rockers CH, sweetie, Teenyweeny EL, Teenyweeny ID, Teenyweeny LC, Teenyweeny RM, Teenyweeny VW, TheNuculearCreeper

Chapter Six

ANobodyZ, barns, Cookieclicker1, Cookieclicker5, Cookieclicker6, Doodleduck, Emerald buddy, Fancyfootball, Lemonspacecurd2, The beak, Twinkle

Chapter Seven

Derpy dog Teenyweeny LMJ, Fancyfootball and Little Boot

Chapter Eight

Booty, Cookieclicker2, croyd123, Derpy dog Teenyweeny LMJ, dog lover, elmo10051, Fancyfootball, gummypie15, Lemonspacecurd1, Lemonspacecurd5, Lemonspacecurd6, Rockers CH, Rockers GW-S, Rockers MP, Rockers SB, santa63, Teenyweeny, Teenyweeny AD, Teenyweeny ID, Teenyweeny KW, Teenyweeny LMJ, Teenyweeny LS, Teenyweeny SP, tiara teenyweeny AJB, TheNucularCreeper

Chapter Nine

Busy Bee Teenyweeny ID, Cookieclicker2, Cookieclicker3, Cookieclicker4, Derpy dog, Teenyweeny LMJ, dog lover, Fancyfootball, Lemonspacecurd1, Lemonspacecurd2, Lemonspacecurd3, Lemonspacecurd5, Rockers ED, Rockers GW-S, Rockers SB, Teenyweeny RM, TheNucularCreeper

Chapter Ten

Cookieclicker1, Cookieclicker4, Cookieclicker5, Cookieclicker7, Fancyfootball, Iceypop Tweenyweeny ALB, Lemonspacecurd1, Lemonspacecurd3, Lemonspacecurd5, Lemonspacecurd6, Lemonspacecurd7, Rockers IM, Teenyweeny AD, Teenyweeny CJ, Teenyweeny LMJ, Teenyweeny TC, Teenyweeny VW

ACKNOWLEDGEMENTS

With the most enormous and heartfelt thanks to:

Julia Iball for so generously providing me with expert mentoring and far more wine than I care to admit to.

Alfie, Bertie, Archie and Annie Beth for putting up with having a writer as a mother and way too many dire dinners.

Gaia Banks for so skilfully steering the Harvey Drew books into print and so generously steering me into restaurants.

Sam Hearn for his awesome and hilarious illustrations.

Cait Davies and Livs Mead at Hot Key Books for their energetic and inventive support.

Sara O'Connor for her excellent editing (as ever) and for choosing *Harvey Drew and the Junk Skunks* to be part of the amazing Story Adventure. But above all, for launching Harvey Drew as Captain of the *Toxic Spew* and for launching me as a writer. Flickering Spew, thank you.

And finally,

All the Story Adventurers for giving me their brilliant ideas and lots of laughs!

Cas Lester

Cas spent many years having a fabulous time, and a great deal of fun, working in children's television drama with CBBC. She developed and executive-produced lots of programmes including *Jackanory*, *Muddle Earth*, *The Magician of Samarkand*, *Big Kids* and *The Story of Tracy Beaker*.

Her programmes have been nominated for numerous awards, including BAFTAs, Royal Television Awards and Broadcast Children's Awards.

Now she's having a fabulous time, and a great deal of fun, writing books for children, helping out in a primary school library and mucking about with her family. She has four children and a daft dog called Bramble. She would absolutely love to go into space. But not on the *Toxic Spew*.

Cas loves doing school visits, so ask your teacher to get involved! To find out more, or just to keep an eye on what Cas is up to, you can visit her at: http://www.caslester.com/
or on Twitter: @TheCasInTheHat

Thank you for choosing a Hot Key book.

If you want to know more about our authors and what we publish, you can find us online.

You can start at our website

www.hotkeybooks.com

And you can also find us on:

We hope to see you soon!